MINE TO PROTECT

CYNTHIA EDEN

CHAPTER ONE

She'd escaped again. *Sonofabitch*. FBI Special Agent Victor Monroe was getting real tired of chasing his prey all around the country. When he put the woman in a safe house, she was supposed to stay...*in the freaking safe house*. She wasn't supposed to vanish and give the agents assigned to guard her a heart attack.

But he'd learned that Zoe Peters rarely did what she was *supposed* to do. The woman made his life far too difficult. As if he didn't already have enough trouble to deal with each day.

Sighing, Victor stared at the bus station. It was nearing midnight and this little town in Kansas...it was not where he wanted to be. A chill brushed over his cheeks. Winter was definitely in the air, and instead of being curled up somewhere, relaxing...

He'd been called after her. Again.

Only this time, things are changing. I don't have the luxury of waiting any longer. I have to act...so I hope Zoe is ready.

He headed into the station, stomping his boots. He wasn't wearing his customary suit. Instead, Victor was clad in old jeans, a sweatshirt, and a thick coat. As soon as he stepped inside that station, he was aware of the silence. Thick, total.

Most of the folks in there appeared to have fallen asleep as they waited for the next bus to arrive, a bus that he knew was scheduled to appear at 12:30 a.m. Zoe thought she'd be on that bus. She was wrong.

She isn't getting away from me.

His gaze scanned the terminals. He was looking for Zoe's dark hair. Sometimes, she wore wigs to disguise herself. As if a different hair color would make her blend into the background any place. Zoe was the kind of woman who always stood out from the crowd.

His attention shifted a bit to the right and to the long bench that waited in the corner. Someone was on that bench — a figure wearing a dark knit cap and one big, majorly oversized coat. That coat completely hid the person's body.

His eyes narrowed as he strode toward that bench. And as he got closer —

A pair of unforgettable green eyes peeked up — met his for just an instant — then hurriedly glanced away.

Oh, Zoe, I have so got you.

He almost smiled.

She seemed to curl in on herself a bit more as he approached, and Victor wondered just what tactic she was going to try using this time.

He sat down on the bench next to her. Before he spoke, he looked around the station once more. He truly wasn't in the mood for a scene — hopefully, she wouldn't create one. There were about ten guys in that place, maybe five women. All of varying ages. He'd prefer to slip out without anyone getting too good of a glimpse of Zoe.

So I'll need to distract folks. Give them something else to remember — something other than her face.

"Sweetheart..." Victor murmured as he turned to face her. "What are you doing?" He kept his voice as low as possible.

Zoe's head tipped up a bit. The cap was pulled down so low that it nearly touched her dark brows. Her green eyes studied him with both anger and fear. Hell, he hated Zoe's fear. Didn't she get that by now? Her lips were wide, full, unpainted, and so sexy that he thought about them far too often.

That was Zoe, though. Walking temptation. Probably the reason she'd been such a hit as a Vegas showgirl. The woman's face was a work of art. At least, as far as he was concerned, it was. Wide eyes, delicate nose, curving chin, high cheekbones — and those sexy lips.

She had long legs. Victor was sure those legs could high kick up a storm. And she was curved in all of the right places — places that were currently hidden by her massive coat.

"Do *not* sweetheart me," she whispered back to him. "Leave me alone. Just walk out of here and let me go."

Victor sighed again and stretched his right arm out along the bench, letting his fingers toy with the edge of her coat. "You know I can't do that."

She growled. The woman would probably freak if she knew he found that sound sexy.

"I am *not* staying locked up any longer!" Zoe said. "You can't make me, *Agent* Monroe."

He heard the rumble of a bus, coming around the station for pickup. It looked as if he'd arrived just in the nick of time. Getting her out of the station would be much easier than hauling her sweet ass off a bus. And it would be less memorable, too.

"Easy or hard?" Victor asked her.

She shot to her feet.

Okay, he figured that meant she'd decided to go with the hard option. Fair enough.

She was trying to hurry toward the boarding area.

He rose, pushed back his shoulders and called out, "Sweetheart, I am so sorry." Victor made sure that his voice was plenty loud and would reach everyone in that room.

Zoe froze.

"I was an ass. An absolute, unforgiveable ass." He walked toward her. Her back was still to him—and to everyone else in the station. Good. "But I swear, baby, I will spend the rest of my life making things up to you."

"*Aw, isn't that sweet?*" The gray-haired lady to his left said, grinning.

Victor gave her what he figured would look like a hopeful smile in return. Hopeful, but not cocky.

Then he focused on Zoe. A still unmoving Zoe. *Oh, but I bet she is pissed right now.* He'd have to deal with that rage soon enough. For the moment, his priority was getting them out of the bus station.

He put his hand on Zoe's shoulder. Zoe's rather puffy shoulder. That coat was almost hilariously huge on her. "Will you forgive me?" Once again, his voice carried easily.

But hers…

"Never," Zoe whispered. Her voice only reached him.

"Oh, thank you, baby!" Victor cried out. He spun her around—fast—and lowered his head over hers. He made sure to cover her with as much of his body as possible and then—

Victor kissed her.

For the scene, of course. Because he had to make things look real for his audience.

And not, *not* because he'd wanted to taste Zoe. Definitely not because of that reason. He was a professional. An FBI agent who took his job seriously.

He was just doing a very, very thorough job, that was all.

Such bullshit.

Her mouth was so soft and silken beneath his, and her lips had parted — probably because the woman had been preparing to rip him a new one. His lips pressed to hers and his tongue slid inside her mouth.

This might be my only shot. I really hope she doesn't slap me.

But…she didn't.

She didn't slap him. She didn't jerk away. Maybe she was too shocked to attack.

So he kissed her deeper. Harder. He let go of the control that he had to always keep in place — so tiring, being in control all the time. Some days, he just wanted to let go.

He wanted to let his darker side out to play. It had been far too long since he'd gone wild.

Her tongue teased his and his cock jerked in eagerness. *She wants me? She wants —*

Her hands were around his shoulders. Her nails bit into his skin. He pulled her closer and mentally cursed that giant jacket because he wanted to feel *her* against him. Not that mound of cushion. A growl built in his throat. He was pretty sure his zipper was making a permanent indention on his growing dick.

Want more. Want her so badly.

But not in a bus station. Not with people gaping at them.

Time to end this scene.

Zoe must have thought the same thing because her nails weren't sinking into him any longer. She was pushing against him.

In a fast swoop, he picked her up in his arms. He hoped that shit looked romantic to everyone who was watching. They'd remember a quarreling couple who made up — and hurried outside.

Not an FBI agent. Not an ex-showgirl on the run.

Reunited lovers.

She had stiffened in his arms, and he tightened his grip as he hauled ass for the door — with her held securely against him. He knew she wouldn't want to make a scene, either, and he'd been counting on that fact.

Zoe knew she was being hunted — and not just by him. A low profile was key for her survival.

A few moments later, they were outside. His breath created a small cloud as the cold air hit him.

"Put. Me. Down." Her voice was way colder than the chill in the air. But he didn't put her down, not yet. Victor didn't lower her until he was standing right beside the rented SUV that he'd used to track her. Once they were at the vehicle—and safely away from prying eyes—he lowered Zoe to her feet and he trapped her between his body and the SUV. The better to stop her from fleeing.

"Why in the hell did you kiss me?" Zoe demanded.

They were both in the shadows, but he could see that her cap had slipped back, letting thick locks of her dark hair tumble free. "It seemed like a good idea at the time," he said.

Her index finger jabbed into his chest. "It was a crappy idea!"

"Really? Because I'm betting if they're pressed, not one of the people in there would be able to describe your face. They weren't focusing on what you looked like, they were focusing on what we were doing."

And she'd sure tasted even better than he'd expected.

His expectations had been high…with her, they always were.

He eased back and opened the passenger side door for her.

She didn't get in. "Why do you keep doing this to me?"

"Protecting you?" He shrugged. "It's sort of my job."

"No, it's not." But she got in the vehicle. A minor miracle. He slammed the door and hurried around to the driver's side. He knew there was a chance she would cut and run from the SUV the minute his back was turned. Luckily, when he jumped in the ride, she was still in the passenger seat. A small miracle.

"Your job," Zoe announced, her voice husky and sensual even when she was pissed, "is not to keep me your prisoner."

"Of course not." He started the ignition. "My job is to keep you alive, though we both know that."

"*Victor.*"

He threw the vehicle into reverse. "Sweetheart, you're a wanted woman. On the lists of more hitmen than I can count. Your dear old dad was one Grade A sadistic bastard before he got thrown in prison, and all of his enemies want to take out their fury on *you.*"

She was silent. Never a good sign from Zoe.

"The FBI wants you alive. We're here to protect you." He turned the vehicle toward the exit.

"There is no *we,*" she huffed out the words. "There is you. You are sitting next to me. You're the jerk who won't let me just vanish. And that's what I want—I can disappear and you can be done with me. I know I've been a pain in your ass—I've tried to be. It's sort of been my whole life goal lately."

Yes, she had been a pain. Always slipping away, never following the simple rules he had in place for her.

"Just let me go." Now her voice had turned pleading. He hated it when she pleaded. Mostly because when she asked him for things, he had a real hard time saying no to her. "I heard…I heard you'd started spreading the word that I was dead, anyway."

He had. Mostly because the heat had just kept coming toward her. So he'd figured if the right people thought she was dead, then she would be safer.

"They think I'm dead." She leaned toward him. Her hand closed around his on the steering wheel. "If they think that, then I can be free."

Only that story was recently blown to hell. "Yeah, about that…" Victor began.

But he didn't get to say another word. Because the windshield on Zoe's side of the vehicle suddenly seemed to explode.

"Zoe!" He bellowed her name even as he slammed his foot down harder on the gas pedal. She slumped near him, and he was fucking terrified that she'd been hit.

He looked at the broken glass and realized—
A bullet. Some sonofabitch had taken a shot at her.

Because despite what Zoe had just said, no one thought she was dead. That wonderful plan he'd had before? A rat at the FBI had turned that plan on its damn head. Now she was being hunted again and if that bullet had hit her…

I will fucking kill that shooter.

He yanked the wheel to the left, then took a hard right, sending them rushing away from the bus station. He wasn't about to stop and give the shooter another chance to fire at her. They were getting the hell out of there.

Another bullet hit the back of the SUV.

Zoe was still slumped low, nearly in his lap.

"Zoe! Talk to me!" Was his heart beating? He wasn't sure. Just breathing was hard. Zoe couldn't be hurt. She couldn't be dead. That shit was not happening. No, no, *no.* A black rage built in him, swallowing up everything in its path and—

"Stop yelling my name and just drive!" Her head turned, just a bit, in his lap. "Because I am staying low until we are away from that jerk! No way am I taking a bullet!"

A smile yanked his lips up and he did just what the lady had ordered—he drove hell fast and he got them the hell away from that jerk.

***

Had he hit her?

Slowly, Kyle Lawrence lowered his weapon. Frustration boiled in his gut. He was a first class sniper, trained by Uncle Sam back during the days when Kyle had been intent on being all he could be...

He didn't normally miss a target. But...
Had she moved? Right before I fired?

Kyle feared she had. And since this particular gig was payable only when the woman's dead body was delivered...hell, he wasn't about to get his payday yet.

He put the rifle back in its case. The weapon had been equipped with a silencer and no one had been outside to witness that little shoot-out. As far as the rest of the world was concerned, the little attack had never even happened. It was so easy to hide most of his hits. Folks never realized the danger that was right around them.

He snapped his rifle case closed and hurried toward his truck. While the FBI agent had been inside, sweet-talking the woman into coming out with him, Kyle had put a tracker on the guy's SUV. The agent wouldn't get far.

And the woman?

If his bullet *had* missed her, well, she still wouldn't live long. Kyle had a reputation to maintain. When he took a hit, he always, *always* got the job done.

Zoe Peters was a dead woman walking. The other fools who *thought* they'd get the bounty on her head? They needed to get in line behind him. She was his prize, and no one would stand in his way.

Not any other fool hit man.

And sure as hell not some FBI agent.

Kyle cranked his truck, floored the baby, and got on the trail of his precious prize.

CHAPTER TWO

I'm alive. I'm alive. I'm alive. Zoe kept chanting those words in her mind. She'd actually felt that bullet whip past her before it sank into the headrest—a headrest that her head had been in front of just seconds before! But she'd leaned toward Victor a split-second before the bullet exploded through the windshield. She'd grabbed his hand...

And managed to stay alive based on sheer, blind luck.

The SUV stopped.

Stopped.

Her head was currently in Victor's lap—yes, a weirdly intimate spot but she didn't care how embarrassing that position was—it was a safe place, and she was all about safety. But when the SUV stopped, her hand clenched around his thigh. A very strong thigh. "What are you doing?"

"I'm making sure you're all right."

And he pulled her up.

She swatted at his hands. "I'm fine! I'd be better if you just kept moving!" Her frantic gaze shot around the vehicle. There was a big, round hole in the front windshield, on *her* side of the vehicle. It was dark outside, and she couldn't see much out there. Maybe some twisted trees. An old farmhouse.

His hand rose and he pushed away her cap. She was surprised she'd still been wearing that thing. Her hair tumbled around her shoulders and his fingers moved carefully over her face. Caressing her cheeks, sliding under her chin. Moving down her neck…

"Um, yeah, no bullet holes," Zoe said, clearing her throat. She didn't like it when Victor touched her. His touch made her heart race, made her knees shake, and made her…well, want things that she shouldn't.

Because FBI Special Agent Victor Monroe? He was not a man she should want. He was not a man she should be fantasizing about. He was not a guy who should be on her desire radar at all…

But he was.

And this is how twisted my life has become.

Every single day, she lived in fear. Would another of her father's psycho enemies come after her? Would she get to be tortured by some other maniac because she had to keep paying for dear old dad's sins?

"That was too close." Victor's voice was low, angry. A hard rumble that was oddly sexy. *Right. Like I don't think nearly everything about the guy is sexy.* That was the reason she'd kissed him back at the bus station. She'd fantasized about his mouth for too long and when he'd pulled her close, Zoe had thought...

Oh, why the hell not?

Now she knew why not. Because that kiss had made her want him more. And in the madness of her current life, she didn't have time to want anyone.

Not even her special agent.

Victor Monroe. Victor of the golden, tanned skin. Victor with the incredible blue gaze that she could never forget. Victor — dark and dangerous and *with the FBI.*

The hand that had been gently stroking her suddenly rose and his fingers curled around her chin, forcing her to look up at him. "This is why you can't run. Your life is on the line."

"I thought...you said it was safer...that people believed I was dead..."

"Yeah, well, that was the general idea. I was circulating the idea that you'd been killed, but turns out...someone at the FBI isn't exactly on your side."

Her breath heaved out. "An FBI agent sold me out?"

"I don't know who, not yet, but my boss is working on that."

She jerked away from him. "I have to get away from you." She reached for the door handle.

But Victor caught her wrist and pulled her right back toward him. "You need to stay with me! I'm the one saving your ass!"

"No, you're not." She twisted her wrist, yanked hard, but the guy didn't let go. "You're the one who got me shot at! If you'd just left me in that bus stop, I would have gotten on the bus, driven away, and been all safe and sound. Instead, you played your kissing game—"

"Kissing game?"

"You dragged me out of that place and you got me *shot* at!"

Headlights appeared in the distance—only, not a very *big* distance away. The lights were already illuminating their SUV.

"Um...Victor..." She licked her dry lips. "Why did you stop here?"

"Because it was a secluded spot and I needed to make sure you were safe!"

Those lights were coming closer. "Is that some agent who is supposed to rendezvous with you? Please, tell me it is."

"Fuck." He jumped out of the vehicle.

Wait — why had he jumped out of the SUV?
"Victor!" She lunged into the driver's seat and

shoved her head out of the side of the vehicle—he'd left the door open in his haste. "What are you doing?" Because that other car was coming close, too fast, and Victor was now crawling around under the SUV.

"Got it!" Then he was rolling from beneath the vehicle and—he tossed *something* away into the dark. "SOB tagged my ride, but he won't be following us any longer."

Someone had *tagged* them? She slumped as low down in the front seat as she could. "Tell me that's not the shooter closing in on us."

"You drive." He'd run around the vehicle and leapt into the passenger side. "And I'll keep him busy."

"But—"

Glass shattered. The other driver had stopped. His lights weren't moving, and since the guy wasn't busy driving—*he is shooting at us again!* Zoe stayed slumped behind the steering wheel but she stretched out her leg and shoved the gas pedal down. They lurched forward and as they did—oh, sweet Jesus—Victor was half-way climbing out his window. He was firing *his* gun at the other vehicle.

She just kept a death-grip on the wheel and prayed that they'd both make it out of that shoot-out alive.

Each time he fired, it sounded like thunder, echoing through the vehicle.

"Don't slow down!" Victor bellowed.

She wasn't planning to slow down — and definitely not planning to stop.

"I got his tires. The bastard won't be following us any time soon." He slid back in the SUV, fully back in. "I'll call my team and get them to pick him up ASAP."

Right. Wonderful. Call in the team. She drove straight ahead, now on a narrow country road, and Zoe had no idea of where she was headed.

"I can't risk going back with you to try and contain him," Victor said. "I don't know what kind of firepower that guy has in his ride, and I don't want to put you at risk."

Did he think she was going to argue? "Call in your team. Let them handle him." The last thing she wanted was to have some kind of face-off with the guy back there.

So Victor yanked out his phone and talked to his team. She drove like a bat out of hell. Zoe kept glancing back in the rearview mirror. No other headlights appeared. The road was empty and she *should* have started to feel safe.

She didn't. Zoe actually couldn't remember the last time that she'd felt safe.

Had it been before she'd first been abducted? Because that was how her *relationship* with Victor had begun. She'd been abducted and held in the dank basement of some rundown house. A guy named Hugh Rowe had taken her, as part of some big elaborate revenge plan that he'd created against her father. Hugh had kept her prisoner, threatened her, *hurt* her.

She'd been sure that Hugh intended to kill her. After all, he'd strapped a bomb to her chest. She'd been so very certain that death was coming for her—

And then Victor had appeared.

We got out of that mess. We survived. How many more escapes do we have left?

Cats had nine lives. She was pretty sure she'd used up far more than nine already. How much longer could this really go on? How many more times was she supposed to escape death?

"Zoe?" Victor said her name softly.

She still flinched.

"Zoe, do you want me to drive?"

When had he gotten off the phone? She blinked and realized that she might be crying. How embarrassing. She hadn't even been aware of the tears sliding down her cheeks. "No…no, I don't want to stop."

If she stopped, maybe that guy would come—

"He's out of commission. My team will be swarming on his location soon. You're safe."

She laughed and the sound was so bitter, even to her own ears.

As she drove, she could feel the weight of Victor's stare on her, but Zoe didn't glance his way. "What would it take," she asked him, aware that her voice was even huskier than normal, "for you to just let me go? I mean…I'd give you anything you wanted."

"Letting you go isn't an option, you know that."

No, she didn't know it. "I've never deliberately hurt anyone. I paid my taxes. I went to school. I had a job. I didn't break any laws…*I didn't do anything wrong.*" But she was still being hunted. Still being kept a prisoner.

"I know." His voice was softer, gruffer. "Sometimes, we're just dealt fucking bad hands by fate."

She swiped the back of her hand over her wet cheeks. "What would you know about a bad hand? I bet you grew up with some kind of silver spoon in your mouth. You probably never had to worry about anything or anyone. I bet —"

"For someone who lived in Vegas for so long, your bets are shit."

Now she did toss a fast glance his way.

"One day, I'll tell you about the way I grew up. The fights and the blood and the lines *I* crossed."

Mr. Follow-The-Law had crossed lines? What lines?

"But that day isn't today. Today, we're going to keep driving for forty minutes and then we're seeking refuge at a safe house."

Not another one.

"It's more of a safe motel," he muttered. "But it's been vetted, and we're crashing there so that I can get a full report from my team."

He meant so that he could hand her off to another team member. Because that was his usual MO. Swoop in. Stop her from vanishing. Pass her off.

"I'm sick of being passed off." Her hands tightened on the wheel. "Why don't you ask me the reason I was getting on that bus? Why don't you ask me—"

"Fine. Why were you getting on that bus?"

"Because my friend needs me." The words exploded out of her. "You know my friend Michelle Lane has been missing—missing *too long.*" She'd gone to Vegas weeks ago to try and find Michelle, but the woman hadn't been there. "She was my only friend. I know someone took her to get to me. I know—"

"FBI agents are searching for her." His fingers were tapping against the door panel. "I told you that when I got you in Vegas."

When he'd swooped in…and passed her off yet again. "That isn't good enough. It's been too long. I'm worried that she's dead." Just saying that fear aloud hurt. "I have to find her. So if you pass me off to another agent, well, guess what? I'll break and run again. I will keep running until I know where Michelle is. Until I know what happened to her. Until I find my friend. Dead or alive."

Okay, wow, she'd gotten a little passionate there. Passionate and loud but she was not going to be passed along again.

He wasn't speaking.

"Say something," Zoe ordered. "Say —"

"If the agents searching aren't good enough, then *I'll* be the one to personally help you."

She shook her head, pretty sure she'd misheard.

"I'll help you," he said again. "But you'll have to help me, too, okay, Zoe? You were promising me *anything* before, weren't you?"

Um… "Yes."

"Then I think you and I will be able to work out a deal."

Her heart stuttered in her chest.

"Keep driving, Zoe," he told her. "Everything is going to be all right."

Was she really supposed to believe those words?

***

Lauren McDaniel didn't want to screw up her first assignment. She'd busted ass to join the FBI, and the last thing she wanted to do was start off her Bureau career with a screw up but…

Her hand tightened on her gun. "The guy isn't here."

She and her partner, Russell Aiker, had made it to the location Victor had given them — they'd gotten there in near-record time. When they'd arrived, the truck had been exactly where Victor had said but...

No driver. The shooter — he's gone. She glanced up at the dark line of trees. "You think he headed out on foot?"

Russell was at the back of the truck. "No. I think the guy just took a back-up ride and hauled ass." He shone his flashlight down at the ground — and there, in the dirt, was the clear impression of a wheel. "Motorcycle," he said, his voice flat. "Probably had it in the back of his truck. This guy was definitely planning ahead. If one ride was disabled, he wanted to be ready to continue his pursuit."

Lauren swallowed. "He sounds —"

"Professional. Yeah, all the guys after Zoe are." He had his phone out. "Better call Victor. The guy is going to be pissed."

Lauren bit her lower lip. Having Victor Monroe pissed was *not* the way she'd wanted to start the job.

"And...just so you're aware...when you meet Zoe Peters, it's a good idea to handle the woman with kid gloves. Even if she does manage to piss you off." He laughed roughly. "'*Cause it will happen.*"

She blinked. "Why the kid gloves?"

"Let's just say Victor doesn't like it when Zoe gets upset."

"But—"

"You upset Zoe, and you will find your ass reassigned. Hell, how do you think you got this gig in the first place?"

She'd had no clue.

"Kid. Gloves." He put the phone to his ear. "Vic? Yeah, we're out here but…no, you aren't going to be happy…"

***

Kyle watched the agents as they searched his truck. He had his night vision goggles on, so he could monitor them. They were standing by his abandoned truck. Just out there, no cover at all. If he'd wanted, he could have taken them both out.

But their deaths wouldn't have helped him. He also wasn't getting paid to off them so…why bother?

He'd taken out his motorcycle. Left a path that made it look as if he'd driven back to the road. Then he'd stayed near the tree line. Gotten cover. He'd wanted to wait and see what the clean-up team looked like.

He'd also wanted to use that team.

Because sooner or later…those two out there would lead him to Victor Monroe. Kyle knew that with certainty. And as he'd already learned that night…

If Victor is around, then Zoe has to be close by. The rumors he'd heard about those two had to be true. And the words he'd just heard the FBI agent say — damn, didn't that guy realize sound carried at night? — they just backed up what he'd already suspected.

Victor Monroe had a personal involvement in Zoe's case. That was why she was such a priority for him. Kyle knew exactly what Zoe looked like, so it wasn't a big surprise to him that Victor was screwing her.

She was hot.

But she wasn't a woman worth dying for. Victor should learn that shit, before it was too late.

CHAPTER THREE

As far as motel rooms went…Victor knew the place they were in pretty much counted as a dump. Definitely the no-tell-motel variety. The bed was sagging, the desk was scarred and wobbly, the door to the bathroom wouldn't close completely, and the carpet was thread-bare.

A dump.

But…at least the dump had a clean bed. He'd made sure of that. Victor had paid extra for fresh bedding because he hadn't wanted Zoe sleeping on someone else's dirt. He'd wanted to make the best of the place for her.

He was always wanting to make things better for Zoe. A weakness, an *issue* that he had. But there was just something about the woman that got to him.

Maybe it was her eyes. The first time he'd looked into them, he'd almost thought he'd lost part of his soul. But then he'd remembered…he'd given up his soul long ago. He cleared his throat. "Sorry about…this."

Zoe gave a faint laugh as she glanced over at him. "Don't worry, Special Agent. I wasn't expecting the Ritz." She dropped the massive coat she'd been carrying around. "I've stayed in worse rooms. Better ones, too, but definitely worse." She sat on the edge of the bed. It gave a long, low groan, and her eyebrows shot up.

He didn't want her staying in that place—he would have fucking loved to put her up at the Ritz, but they were in the middle of freaking nowhere, and their options for a safe place to crash were severely limited. No questions were asked at this motel, and he'd been given the room on the far end—the most private one. One that also provided him with a view of anyone who might try to come his way.

A safe enough place, for the night. They'd been signed in under fake names, a married couple. And the motel sign-in log had been full of other fake names.

Celebrities. Dead presidents. Plenty of interesting names had been on that list at the front desk.

"So I heard you talking to your FBI buddies," Zoe murmured. "He got away, huh?" She wasn't laughing now and her gaze held fear.

He hated her fear, and he hated having to say, "Yeah, he was gone."

She nodded. "So I guess he's still on the hunt."

He was...and other hitmen were out there, too. "The bounty on your head just keeps rising."

Zoe glanced away from him. Her stare went to the little TV that was on a stand near the foot of the bed. Judging by the look of it, Victor figured that TV hadn't worked in years.

"So many people hate Luther," Zoe mused. "And they never seem to think...I hate him, too. I want him to pay, too. It's not like Luther Bates will win the award for Father of the Year." Her eyes closed. "Everyone knows he was a monster. So what the hell do people think he was like when I was a kid?"

He'd been curious about her life with Luther, but she hadn't told Victor jackshit before. He leaned against the wall, crossed his arms over his chest, and wondered if this was the turning point for them. Was she finally lowering the wall she'd kept up? Finally *trusting* him?

"At first, when I was younger, I wondered why he hadn't married my mom." Her eyes opened and she turned her head, meeting his gaze. "That's what a five-year-old wonders, you see. Why don't mom and dad live together? Is something wrong?"

He waited, silent.

"When I was ten, when I barely saw him at all, I thought...we're his dirty little secret. He's ashamed of me. Of my mom. So he keeps us away from everyone else. He doesn't take us out to dinners or on trips. He doesn't come to my school to see my plays because he's embarrassed. *I've* embarrassed him. I'm a disappointment. That's what a ten year old thinks." Her lips curved down as sadness chased over her face.

You aren't a disappointment. You could never be a disappointment.

"Then, when I was fifteen…I saw his face on the news. I wondered…why is my dad on the news? And then…then I heard what the reporter was saying. That he was a criminal. A killer. That he was some kind of suspected mob boss. My mom was in the room with me, watching the news, and she was crying. That was when I knew…"

When her voice trailed off and Zoe didn't continue, Victor waited a moment, then pushed, "When you knew what?"

"That my father was a monster. My mother was always so careful around him because she was *terrified* of him. And he kept us hidden because…" Now her laughter came once more. Sad. Painful. "Because he knew we would be targets. He knew people would hurt us in order to get to him. That's what his world was, you see. The *an-eye-for-an-eye* mentality ruled there. Survival of the fittest dominated. Good and evil—those concepts didn't matter at all."

"You confronted your father. About what he…was." This was the part he needed. He had to learn what secrets Zoe had been keeping. And he suspected there were plenty of secrets.

"Of course, I confronted him. When you're fifteen, you think you can change the world." Her smile stretched. "You think that maybe you can still get the happy life you always dreamed of. You think you can change the monster."

Nothing will change Luther Bates. Victor had spent too many hours staring into that man's cold, dead eyes. Luther was evil. Pure and fucking simple. Luther had ordered the deaths of so many people...and never even hesitated. "What happened?"

She pushed off the bed, rising to her feet. "Oh, the usual. My crime boss father instantly became good and charming. Everything that a girl could wish her father to be." Zoe hurried toward the bathroom. "I need to shower."

He moved, blocking her path. "What happened?"

She lifted her chin and stared into his eyes. "You've met Luther, haven't you? Stared at him, face to face?"

Yes.

"I told him that he had to stop. That he couldn't keep doing those terrible things." Her breath whispered out. "At first, he laughed at me."

"Zoe..."

"And then he hit me so hard that I flew across the room."

Fucking hell. Victor's hands fisted.

"I got a concussion. Six stitches in the back of my head." She shrugged. "Apparently, no one questions Luther Bates, not even his daughter."

He wanted to touch her. So badly. He also wanted to beat the ever loving hell out of her father.

"My mother saw what he'd done. She'd always been there for him, smiling so brightly when he appeared at the door, only waiting to cry when he left. But that day, when she picked me up from the floor and my blood was on her hands, she stopped smiling for him." Her voice lowered with each word she spoke. "She told him to leave. Not to come back." Her lashes fell, shielding her eyes. "Luther Bates doesn't like to be told no."

He thought of Zoe's file. *Fifteen. She'd been fifteen and —*

Hell.

"If you read my file, you'll know that my mother…she was…killed in a home invasion. That attack happened just a few days after she told Luther to stay away from us."

Had Luther ordered the attack? Paid for it to look like—

"Two months after her death, Luther shipped my ass off to boarding school. Some fancy ass place where I didn't belong. But at least I wasn't with him anymore."

Holy fucking hell. Just what had happened during those two months that she spent with her father? He sucked in a deep breath and tried to figure out where he should push the hardest. *The mother. Start there.* "You had to know your mother's death was suspicious."

She gave a broken laugh. "Trust me, I knew plenty."

Tell me plenty, sweetheart. Tell me. "Did he ever admit it to you? Did he ever tell you —"

"That he had my mother killed?" Her voice was just a rasp now. Her lashes lifted. She gazed up at him, and there was so much pain in her eyes. "There was no need to tell me. The police report said it was a home invasion. But I was *there.*"

Tell me. It was his job to get the truth from her. His hands were still fisted at his sides. Fisted so hard they hurt. *Touch her. Hold her. Take away her fucking pain.* Only right then, he was the one putting her in pain as he made her dig up her bloody past.

"My mother was one of the only people who actually loved him." A tear slipped from her eye.

Oh, hell, I cannot handle her tears. "Zoe…"

"I need to shower," she said again, voice tight. "Please, I-I need to shower."

You need to tell me. Give me nails to shove in Luther's coffin.

She pushed past him and ran into the bathroom. She shoved that door closed — as much as it would shut.

Victor stared at that white door and its peeling paint. He knew he couldn't press her anymore, not right then. He had a job to do — one he didn't like. One Zoe didn't fully understand. Getting her to trust him, getting her to confide all in him — yeah, that was the plan. The big order from up top at the Bureau.

But right then, Zoe had been through enough. She'd nearly died — right beside him — that night. Fear was still present, curling like a snake in his gut. He wasn't used to fear. There were only two people in the world he cared about. Two people that weren't family, not really, but fate and circumstance had bonded them so that they were *better* than family. Saxon Black and Jasmine Bennett. Though Bennett wasn't the name she used any longer…Long ago, he, Saxon and Jasmine had forged a life together on the streets. Helped each other. Supported one another.

Kept each other's secrets.

He'd feared for them before. Been worried as all hell about their survival. But Saxon and Jasmine *had* beaten the threats they faced.

And his fear had faded.

Until Zoe. Until beautiful Zoe Peters had come into his life. Until she'd been threatened. When he'd thought she might be dead in that SUV with him, something had changed. The fear had come barreling back, only it had been so much worse than any terror he'd ever experienced before.

The fear hadn't faded, not completely, and he knew it was because Zoe still wasn't safe.

Zoe was getting under his skin. The plan had been for her to connect with him. Not for him to feel this stupid fucking tie with her. But...

It's there. Her pain hurts me.

He headed toward the bathroom door. He could hear the roar of the shower inside. He put his hand on the door. "Zoe, do you need anything?"

There was no response. His hand moved to the doorknob. Was she crying in there? Was she—

"Just leave me alone, Victor." Her voice was soft and so very sad.

His hand stilled on the knob. *I wish I could, baby. I wish I could...but that isn't going to happen.*

***

Zoe needed clothes. When she'd been fleeing to the bus station, she hadn't exactly stopped to pack an extra bag. Her priority had been to get away from the FBI agent, Russell Aiker, who'd been guarding her. So she'd pretty much vanished with the clothes on her back. Now Zoe stood in the middle of the bathroom, her hair wet and a towel wrapped around her body. The mirror in front of her was too fogged up for Zoe to see her own reflection. That last bit was probably a good thing—she didn't want to look at herself right then.

After all this time, and, yes, looking in my own eyes is still too hard. Because she didn't like what she saw in the mirror. Didn't like it at all.

Luther's daughter.

Maybe she'd just put back on the clothes she'd worn before. She could do that. The long sleeved t-shirt and jeans would be fine for now. Far better to wear them than to prance around in front of Victor just wearing a towel.

That would be such a bad idea. *As bad as sharing a motel room with him tonight?* Because Victor had only booked one room. One room with one bed.

As if her night had not been bad enough.

She heard a sharp knock—one that had her head jerking to the right. Only the knock wasn't on the bathroom door. The sound had been too distant. *Someone is outside of our motel room.*

"Relax, Zoe," Victor called out. As if he'd known she'd just gotten scared as all hell. "It's my team."

Good. Fabulous. His team. Not the current killer on her trail. And with more FBI agents there—their presence definitely meant it was time to put her clothes back on. She dressed as quickly as she could, not bothering with her shoes, but wearing her underwear, jeans and that t-shirt. Then she yanked open the bathroom door.

The group was waiting near the bed. Victor, looking confident and grim—his usual style. Victor's dark hair wasn't even tousled. His blue eyes glinted, and his broad shoulders were set with determination. Russell—he wore his suit, unwrinkled, *his* usual perfect style. Russell Aiker was a tall, handsome, African American in his early thirties. She actually *liked* Russell. And he seemed to like her, too. That was how she'd been able to give him the slip before. *Don't make the mistake of being kind to me. I use kindness.*

"Hi, Zoe," Russell murmured, his mouth lifting in a half-smile. "Glad to see you're still alive."

"Glad to still be alive." Her gaze slid to the right. Ah, a new agent. A woman with blonde hair that fell to her chin and brown eyes that were assessing as they slid over Zoe, lingering just for a moment on...

My bare toes.

Zoe wiggled her toes. Then she nodded toward the woman. "Hello." *Hello, fresh meat.*

The woman nodded briskly in response. "I'm Agent Lauren McDaniel." Lauren straightened her shoulders. "I believe I'm here to take over watch duty." Her gaze slid to Victor. "I'll make sure she doesn't leave tonight."

Agent Lauren McDaniel was there to do what now? Zoe marched right into that circle of agents. "Sorry, but there is a huge mistake happening here." She took up a position near Victor. She knew he was the lead agent in that room. And he was the one who'd made a deal with her. She wasn't going with Agent Fresh Meat anywhere. The woman sure wasn't about to become her bunkmate for the night. "I'm not in the market for a new guard."

Russell winced a bit. *Right, sorry. I ran out on him last night.* She cast a quick, apologetic glance his way.

"Do you have a death wish, ma'am?" Lauren asked her, voice tight.

Zoe's eyes widened.

"*I warned her,*" Russell muttered.

"Because I have read your file," Lauren continued doggedly, "and I know all about the risks you have taken. You keep running from us, when all we want to do is keep you safe. But how are we supposed to adequately do our jobs when you fight us every step of the way?" Lauren nodded toward Zoe. "You should be grateful for our assistance. You should be—"

Zoe held up her hand. "I love it when people tell me what I should be. Truly, one of my favorite things in life." She was not liking Fresh Meat. Zoe turned to face Victor. "I thought we had an agreement." A very recent agreement. "What happened to that deal? Are you seriously turning me over to blondie there?"

His gaze was guarded. She hated that. Why was he always hiding his emotions from her?

"That's your usual MO," Zoe threw at him, growing angrier with every second that passed. "Stop me from fleeing — like I want — stop me from getting on with my life. Bring me back to some safe house. Hand me off to another agent. Then vanish…"

"And your MO is to start the cycle all over," Victor responded. "To lull the new agent into a false sense of security. To act like you're following the rules. Then as soon as the agent's attention shifts away, you run."

Her shoulders lifted, then fell. "A girl has to do what a girl has to do." She wasn't apologizing. She'd told him *exactly* why she'd been at the bus station. Michelle. Michelle was *still* missing.

Even before the FBI had pulled Zoe into their web, she and Michelle had been using a secret way of staying in contact with one another. They'd set up calls — once a month. Check-in calls. She'd snuck away from her FBI guards a few times to make those calls. And at first, everything had been fine…

Then Michelle stopped answering. When Michelle hadn't responded for two months, Zoe had become desperate. She'd started reaching out to old contacts. Only…*the word from my contacts in Vegas is that no one knows where Michelle went. She vanished…*

I have to find her.

"There isn't any more running," Victor said, his voice gruff. Then he looked over her shoulder, focusing on the two watching agents. "Zoe and I have a new deal. For the foreseeable future, I'll be the agent on Zoe's guard duty."

"*You?*" Lauren sounded as if she were choking. "But sir—"

Zoe turned back to look at her, frowning. "But what? You don't think he can watch me? That's just insulting to the man."

"Zoe…" Victor whispered.

"Well, it is." She lifted her chin. "Victor is on guard duty with me. You heard him. He'll be my twenty-four, seven companion. So just rest easy on that one, okay?"

Lauren's gaze jerked to Victor's face.

"I want you and Russell finding the driver of that truck. I know he's still in the area," Victor said grimly. "You need to find him and bring the guy in ASAP because he's not going to stop. He will just keep hunting Zoe until he can claim the bounty on her."

"Him and plenty of others," Russell said.

Russell, that is not helpful.

"Sorry, Zoe," Russell added. *Such a nice guy.* "But you know it's true. The bounty on your head doubled in the last week."

It had — doubled? She took a quick step back and her shoulders hit Victor's chest. His arm came up — instantly — and curled around her.

"Thought you'd already told her." Russell's lips curled down. "Hell."

No, Victor hadn't told her that the price was *double.* "That's two million dollars." Breathing was hard. "Two million dollars for my life?"

"Two million dollars to end your life," Lauren corrected.

Her knees were shaking.

"It's not going to happen," Victor whispered in her ear. "I will keep you safe."

Her head turned toward him. She stared up at him. Their pose was intimate, she knew it, and she didn't care what the other agents thought. "That bullet missed me by inches tonight."

A muscle jerked in his locked jaw.

"How long do I get to keep cheating death?" Sooner or later, she'd be paying...*for the crimes my father committed.*

"Zoe..."

"How does it end?" Because she saw only one way to stop the hitmen on her trail...*one of them takes me out.*

"I *will* keep you safe. I did a fucking poor job tonight, but I will lay down my life for you."

Her heart nearly shot out of her chest. "Is that what you think I want? You dying for me?"

"It's—"

"It's not. I don't want you dying. I don't want Russell dying or even Fresh Meat over there dying. I want you all safe. I don't want this danger put on anyone else. I want it all—I just want it to stop. I want my life to be normal."

Only her life had never been normal.

His arm was still around her. Their bodies were touching. His mouth was close. If she stood on her tip-toes, she'd be kissing him. He was tall, muscled. So sexy to her. And those lips of his...

I want to kiss him. I want him to need me. I want to go wild with Victor and forget everything else.

Only that wasn't happening, either. "I think I'll go to bed." Maybe things would look like less of a nightmare in the morning.

Maybe.

Probably not.

His arm slid away from her.

"Good night, Russell," Zoe murmured. "Good night...um, Agent McDaniel." She quickly made her way to the bed. She heard the floor squeak behind her, and then hinges creak as the door opened.

Their footsteps padded to the door. She glanced over her shoulder and saw Victor, standing in the doorway. The other two agents had already gone out. "I'll just be right outside," he told her. His gaze was still guarded.

One day, I'll get past his guard.

She nodded and he shut the door.

***

Victor stood just outside of the motel room.

Russell gave a low whistle. "You sure this is the path you want to take?"

"I'm sure this is the next step." He'd worked with Russell on plenty of other cases. The guy was a good agent. Sure, Zoe had given him the slip, but she'd managed to sneak away while under the watch of other well-trained agents, too.

The woman was good at escaping. *I'll have to ask her...did she stay in that boarding school until she hit eighteen? Or did she escape from there, too?*

"You're getting involved very...closely with her," Russell added, his voice low, concerned.

The new agent just watched them, her body tense.

"That's the point, isn't it?" Victor gave him a tired smile. Russell knew the score on this case—

the real agenda. Hell, it was why the guy had been so affable with Zoe.

Get her trust. Get her to reveal everything that she knows.

Zoe's case was a very, very unusual beast.

Luther Bates thought he'd blackmailed Victor into watching out for Zoe, keeping her alive, but the truth was…

The FBI planned to use Zoe in order to take down Luther and his empire completely. Luther Bates still had plenty of power, even though he was behind bars. His minions were only too happy to keep carrying out their boss's dirty work. And with that massive team of lawyers that Luther had on call…*the bastard is actually working to get out of prison.*

The FBI couldn't, *wouldn't,* let that happen.

Word had recently reached them that one lawyer in particular was meeting far too frequently with Victor. The crime boss thought he had a way to get out of prison. To get back on the streets.

"Be careful," Russell warned him. "Sometimes, you can lose your soul in this job. You don't want that to happen."

Victor laughed. "Don't worry about that. I lost my soul years ago." When he'd nearly beat a man to death in a fight that *shouldn't* have happened.

Another life.

Another time.

He looked down at his hands. *Still fucking me.* "Use that truck to track down the shooter. Maybe the guy left fingerprints, DNA, something in there..."

"We already have our crime scene techs on the job," Lauren said quickly.

Yeah, he'd figured they'd be busy. "Report to me as soon as you have any news."

Lauren shifted her stance. "If you give me the chance, I can prove myself." Determination flowed in her voice. "I can guard her. Zoe won't be hurt on my watch."

Victor focused on Lauren. "Lauren McDaniel." He said her name thoughtfully. "Do you know that I handpicked you to join the team handling Zoe's case?"

"Ah, no, no, I didn't know that."

"You don't have to prove yourself. Not to me or anyone else. You have the badge. You're in the Bureau. I know you can do the job."

"Then why—"

"Plans have changed," he said before she could ask why he was taking over guard duty— because he knew that had been her question. "I plan to stay personally involved in this case for the foreseeable future. Too much attention is focused on Zoe right now. Until the sharks stop circling in..." Sharks, hitmen—same damn thing. "I'll be at her side."

"Good luck," Russell told him.

Oh, he'd need more than luck.

Because his boss at the Bureau — the fucking assistant director — had told Victor he had to come back with results. Actionable intel from Zoe that they could *use* against her father.

And the assistant director had also told him that if he didn't get what they needed, Victor was supposed to play hardball with Zoe. Supposed to tell her that the FBI would walk away — and leave her ass on her own.

The assistant director is a cold bastard.

One thing Victor knew...he wasn't walking out on Zoe. Not this time — not ever again.

***

Zoe's ear pressed to the glass — a dirty glass she'd found in the bathroom. The glass was pressed to the motel room door, the better for her to eavesdrop on the agents. It had been an old trick, one she'd used when she was a child and she'd wanted to overhear just what her mom and dad were talking about.

On one of those rare visits that Luther made to their apartment...

Her breath barely slipped past her lips as she listened to the murmur of voices outside of the motel room. Victor, Russell, Lauren.

What did Victor mean about losing his soul? The guy had plenty of soul. Sure, he was a bit icy at times but…

Her hold tightened on the glass. *What secrets are you keeping, Victor?*

He dismissed the agents. She heard him tell them goodnight.

Crap. She jumped away from the door. Zoe rushed toward the bed, pausing just long enough to hide the glass under the faded bed skirt. Then she hopped on the bed. The mattress gave that long groan again.

She closed her eyes. Tried to make her body look relaxed. Did her breathing sound even? She hoped her cheeks weren't flushed.

Zoe rolled, turning away from the door and curling her body in a bit. The door creaked open behind her and she heard the heavy tread of Victor's footsteps.

Would he buy that she'd drifted off to sleep? Would he just leave her alone until morning?

His footsteps came closer and—

He walked to the other side of the bed. Clothing rustled. Zoe wanted to crack open one eye and look at him, but that would totally blow her fake sleeping routine to hell.

More rustling. A *lot* of rustling. Just how much was the guy taking off?

Then the bed dipped. *Whoa, whoa, whoa!* There was a perfectly good floor for the man to use. He could *not* be crawling into bed with her.

Her eyes flew open.

And she found him lying right beside her. His gaze was on her face, and Victor was smiling. "Nice try, baby, but I saw the glass peeking out from your side of the bed. Next time, cover it up better." His smile stretched. "Eavesdrop much?"

"Only every chance I get." He was in bed. With her.

His hand reached toward her. He tucked a lock of hair behind her ear. "Zoe Peters…" he murmured. "Just what am I supposed to do with you?"

Everything that we both want. The words were there, rising within her, and it took all of Zoe's strength not to say them out loud.

CHAPTER FOUR

Zoe's hair was still wet. Wet and sleek and she smelled sweet — her scent was wrapping around Victor, teasing him. Seducing him.

No, it was her gaze that seduced. Green eyes that were sensual, tempting.

Their bodies were just inches apart. He wanted to close that space. To put his mouth on hers. To taste her like he wanted — no restraint. No holding back.

Just greed. Lust.

The desire that he was tired of fighting.

Every time he saw Zoe, his need for her grew. It was wrong, he knew that. He should keep his hands off her but —

His fingers trailed over her cheek. Slowly, carefully, his hand moved down. His index finger slid over her plump lower lip. Her lips were parted, just a bit and…his breath left him in a fast whoosh.

She just licked my finger. He'd felt the quick, wet lick of her tongue on his finger. His dick immediately hardened for her. Hardened even more…because he'd been aroused for her before he even climbed into the bed.

"Are we going to keep pretending?" Zoe asked him. When she spoke, her lips moved against his finger and he felt the light caress of her tongue again.

"Pretending?" He wanted her mouth beneath his. Wanted to feel that sexy pink tongue of hers on so many other parts of his body.

Her hand rose and pressed to his chest. He'd ditched his shoes, socks, coat and shirt — and he was wearing just his jeans. So when her hand reached out, her fingers pressed directly to his skin.

"You're warm," Zoe murmured.

Her touch seemed to burn straight to his core.

"I know you want me."

The woman was dead-on with that statement. Wanted her. Was insane for her. Wanted to strip her and fuck her all night long.

"I also know you've been staying hands off. Probably because you're the agent in charge. Mr. Law-Abiding. You don't break rules." Her hand slid lightly over his chest. "You don't cross lines."

There were plenty of lines he wanted to cross with her. So many that the woman would need a safe word.

"So I'm not going to pretend that I can't tell you want me." Her hand dipped a little lower.

Sweet hell. "And I won't pretend that I don't want you, too."

His racing heartbeat thundered in his ears.

"The truth is…I've wanted you for a while, Victor."

She was shattering his control with every low, husky word.

"I've thought about you. Dreamed about you. Been pissed as all hell with you but…I want you. I always do."

Her fingers were on one of his scars. Those freaking scars littered his body. Marks from gunshots. Knife wounds. His time on the streets. He'd always carry those reminders.

Zoe didn't seem repulsed by his scars. Her fingers were so warm and soft against him.

"So I'm telling you how I feel. Exactly how I feel…and now it's your turn."

His turn?

"Do we keep playing by the rules, Victor? Or do we cross some lines?"

"Zoe…" Just saying her name was hard. Desire beat in his blood and his voice came out as a rough growl. "Be very careful…"

"Why? I've tried being careful. It still got me on hit lists. My time is slipping away—"

The hell it was.

"Inches. I was inches away from death tonight. Seems like a real damn shame. To want you this way and to never get to feel—"

He kissed her. He lunged toward her, closed that distance between them, and took her mouth. There was no finesse from him. No careful seduction. He just took because the last thread of his self-control had been shredded by her words.

I've wanted her for too long. To want her, and not to have her...

He was changing the rules. Crossing the line. And he didn't care. All that mattered to Victor right then—Zoe.

Tasting her. Claiming her. Taking her.

Forgetting the fear, banishing that shit. Focusing on the passion. The lust that blazed white-hot.

He rolled her onto her back. He was so glad he'd slipped the clerk an extra fifty to make sure they were in a room with damn clean bedding. Though he wished their first time together was somewhere else.

A fancy hotel. A beach. Some snow-covered inn.

Some place romantic, though he wasn't normally the romantic sort. He just—Victor wanted it for her.

She caught his lower lip and bit it lightly.

Fucking yes.

Her hands slid over him. Pushed down to the top of his jeans. She was fumbling with the button and the zipper, and—

"Baby, not yet." His breath sawed out of his lungs. "You put your hands on my cock, and I'll be lost."

She smiled up at him. "I think I want you lost."

"You're going first." And he was going to enjoy exploring every single inch of her. Victor kissed Zoe again, a deep, hot kiss. She arched up toward him, and he felt the press of her breasts against his chest.

Every single inch of her.

He kissed his way down her neck. Zoe gasped and her nails sank into his sides. He would have smiled at her reaction, but he was too turned on for smiling.

He caught her shirt in his hands, pulled back just a little, and yanked the thing up and over her head. The shirt hit the floor and he stared down at her.

Zoe wore a plain white bra — and it had to be the sexiest thing he'd seen in his life. Her breasts pushed out, spilling against those cups. He bent forward and kissed one breast even as he slid his fingers under the edge of her bra and found her nipple. Tight. Hard.

"*Victor!*"

He loved it when she said his name. And when there was so much desire in her voice…*hell, yes.* But he still had to warn her… "The walls here are thin, baby."

Her eyes widened and she immediately pressed her lips together.

"One day soon, I want you to yell for me. As long as you can."

He unhooked her bra. Perfect breasts. Pink nipples, round and full…and when he licked her, when he sucked her, her hips rocked up against him.

She tastes so good. Like she was made for me. Only me.

His mouth eased down her body. He kissed the curve of her stomach and loved the way she lifted up against him.

"Do something fun," Zoe suddenly whispered when his mouth hovered over her jeans. "Use your teeth to undo the button…"

He looked up. Her eyes were gleaming as she stared at him, and a faint smile curved her lips.

I'm about to fuck Zoe Peters.

And she was making him feel…good. Happy. Making him feel like smiling back at her. His cock was so swollen that the thing hurt. He wanted to plunge balls deep into her and drive them both into oblivion but…

He smiled back at her. And he did something fun, just as she'd ordered. He used his teeth to undo the button of her jeans. Then the zipper slid down with a hiss.

"Guess what else I can use my mouth to do…" He pushed her jeans out of the way. Her panties went down with them. Then he was spreading her legs wide. Positioning her so that he could have full access.

And using his mouth in the very best of ways.

"*Victor!*"

So maybe she didn't care about the thin walls. Neither did he. Right then, all he cared about was her. One lick, and he was addicted to her taste. His mouth pressed to her, his fingers pressed *in* her, and he explored all of her most sensual secrets.

Her hips twisted against him, pushing up harder against his mouth. He could feel the gathering tension in her. Zoe was close to a release—so close, already.

His thumb stroked her clit and she jerked beneath him, coming on a sharp cry of pleasure.

Hell, yes.

He rose back over her. Barely took time to ditch his jeans and grab the condom from his wallet—thank fuck it was still there. He rolled on the condom then put his cock right at the entrance to her body.

But he didn't thrust into her. Not yet.

Her breath was still heaving in and out. Her lashes had lowered but when he paused, those long lashes lifted and her gaze locked on his.

"Ready to cross some lines?" Victor asked her.

She gave a quick nod.

His hands caught hers. Their fingers threaded together, then he pushed her hands back against the pillow.

He thrust into her. Balls-freaking-deep. A groan tore from him because she felt like heaven. Hot. Tight. Perfect.

I crossed the line, and I will never go back.

He withdrew, then thrust into her again. He was too rough, too hard, and the bed was squeaking beneath him. Her legs wrapped around his hips, squeezing him and pulling him so close. She was whispering his name, urging him on, and all he wanted —

He wanted to feel her come with his cock buried deep inside of her.

He angled his hips. Made sure that his length slid over her clit when he drove into her. The pace was frantic, the urge to reach that wild blast of release consuming him.

"Victor!" Not a scream. Her whisper. A cry of satisfaction and he saw the pleasure wash across her face. Her green eyes widened and her cheeks flushed. Her delicate inner muscles clamped along his length, squeezing him as the orgasm rocked through her.

And then he was exploding. His release hit him with the force of a freaking truck. He emptied into her, pleasure shaking his whole body. The climax went on and on, and he kept thrusting, never wanting that moment to end.

Even as the pleasure lashed him, Victor knew he'd made a serious mistake. The worst of his life, probably.

He'd wanted Zoe. He'd needed her. But he hadn't realized…

He hadn't just fucked her. It had been…more.

He'd had sex with other women. Good sex.

This was different. Zoe was different.

She was making everything different for him.

Her lips curled — that slow smile — and that sweet smile of hers that was meant just for him.

It wasn't just fucking. Not with her.

And he was screwed.

But in that moment, Victor couldn't care. He leaned toward her. Kissed her lips. Softly. Lightly. With care.

Emotions were choking him, but his body was more replete than it had ever been. He eased from her. Kissed her once more. Then he padded to the bathroom. While he ditched the condom, he didn't look in the mirror. He didn't want to look at himself, not right then. He turned off all the lights and went back to Zoe.

When he climbed onto the bed, she immediately turned toward him. Taking her into his arms seemed like the most natural thing in the whole world. She put her head on his chest, right over his heart, and his arms closed around her.

He shouldn't have been able to sleep that way. Not so easily. Not to just close his eyes and drift off. He never let down his guard. And cuddling after sex wasn't his usual MO but...

His eyes drifted closed and his hands stayed curled around Zoe as Victor fell asleep.

***

It was the creak of the door that woke Victor, hours later. The little motel room was still dark — no light at all sliding through the thin blinds. His eyes opened when he heard that creak and Victor lunged up in bed.

A bed that only he occupied.

Zoe!

Was she seriously trying to give him the slip? After what they'd done together? Had she just been trying to lure him into some false sense of security with the mind-melting sex so that she could escape from him the second his guard dropped? And it sure as hell had dropped.

He leapt from the bed, naked, and rushed toward the motel room door.

Before he could reach it, Zoe opened the *bathroom* door — it gave a long creak — and when she stepped out, Victor grabbed her arms as he tried to stop from running her down.

"Victor!"

Yeah, they both almost hit the floor with that collision, but he did some fast and frantic footwork, and he managed to keep them upright—barely.

She gave a quick, nervous laugh. "Do you have some sort of issue you need to tell me about? Not sleep walking but like…sleep tackling?"

He didn't laugh. "I thought you'd left."

"Um, no."

His hold tightened on her arms. "I don't want you to leave me." The way she'd ditched the other agents.

Her hair slid over his fingers as she tilted back her head. "I'm not planning to leave you. We have a deal, remember?"

At her soft words, guilt twisted within him.

"Besides, I don't make a habit of leaving a lover without a word in the middle of the night."

Lover.

"And I sure hope," Zoe added a bit darkly, "that you don't, either."

He wished he could see her expression. But she was just a shadow to him and he knew he appeared the same way to her. "Is that what we are now? Lovers?"

"I would think so." She paused. "Lovers and partners."

His hands slowly slid away from her shoulders. From all of that wonderful, smooth skin. "I shouldn't have crossed that line." He backed up. Turned away from her. Tried to figure out how he was supposed to fix things with her. The heat of the moment was one thing, but the aftermath — *sanity comes back.*

"Do *not* act like it was all your decision." Anger beat in her voice. "I wanted you. You wanted me. It was a very mutual thing, I promise you. Screw the lines. Life is short — sometimes, brutally so — we should all take what happiness and pleasure we can."

The problem was that he wanted to take everything from Zoe.

Take and take…

And then he was supposed to just walk away?

His hands clenched as he stood there in the dark. "Do you trust me, Zoe?"

She didn't answer.

Not yet. She doesn't trust me yet. She gave me her body, gave me her desire, but I've still got a long way to go with Zoe.

"Show me that I *can* trust you," Zoe said. He heard her footsteps shuffle closer. "Keep up your end of the deal. Help me to find Michelle. Help me to make sure that she's alive. Get her safe and secure. Then I'll trust you plenty."

He turned back toward her. His eyes had adjusted more to the darkness, but he still couldn't see her expression. "So people have to prove themselves to you?"

"After my life…and the number of users who've swept into it? Yes, yes, I need proof. The days of trusting blindly are long gone for me."

That was what he'd suspected—and what his boss at the Bureau had thought, too. "How many people have betrayed you during your life?"

He heard her suck in a sharp breath, as if his question had hurt her.

"Too many to count."

He rubbed his chest, a chest that had—oddly—just started to ache. Victor paced away from her and jerked on his jeans.

"Want to hear something sad?" Zoe asked him.

He was supposed to learn all of her secrets. But… "I think I'd rather hear something that made you happy."

She came toward him then, a quick tumble of steps. Her arms lifted and wrapped around him. "*You.*"

"What?"

She leaned onto her toes and pressed a quick kiss to his mouth. "You make me happy."

No, not him. He didn't make anyone happy. The other agents were scared of him. His birth family had deserted him and—

"My true blue, always-gets-the-bad-guy agent. *You* make me happy because I know you can't be bought. You're not on my father's payroll. You aren't out to hurt me."

That ache in his chest turned into a burn.

"I had one friend at that boarding school…a quiet girl who was my roommate. We grew really close during my time there. I thought she got me. I thought she cared, and then I found out that she was a plant. Her father *worked* for mine, and she was going back…telling them all my secrets. All about my plans for sneaking away. For starting a new life. She told them everything."

No wonder trust is hard…

"And when I was twenty-one, I thought I was in love. He was a law student, just a few years older than me. Tom was smart, charming, way too handsome."

He hated the dick.

"He was also on my father's payroll. Not that I realized that, of course. I would hardly have dated the guy, have *slept* with him, if I'd known that."

Maybe *hate* wasn't a strong enough word to describe how Victor felt about Tom.

"Can you believe that?" Zoe continued. "My father had *handpicked* the guy he wanted me to marry. A man he could control. Manipulate totally."

Fucking hell. The burn in Victor's chest got worse with every word she spoke.

"I found out that news quite by accident." Her body brushed against Victor's. "That's usually the way I find out. I mean, it's not like people come up to me and say, 'Hi. I'm here to betray you.'"

Fuck, fuck, fuck.

"It was one of those random things with Tom. We were living in Vegas. My father never spent a lot of time there, he was more of an East Coast guy, so I thought I was safe. I went into a restaurant one day—and, bam, Tom was sitting in a back both, looking all cozy as he was chatting up my father. My father," she said again, voice going husky. "One of the coldest human beings in the world. A mob boss. A monster. And Tom was drinking champagne with him."

Don't say another word. Don't say—

"Tom saw me, and instead of being embarrassed or shocked, he called me over. He was celebrating, you see. He'd passed the bar exam, *and* my dad had just given his approval for Tom to go ahead and marry me. Everything was going to be all in the family now." She'd slid back down, and she put her head on his chest, close to the spot that burned. His hands rose. Hesitant, so very hesitant, he hugged her. "Tom was going to take his place in my father's organization. I was going to be the good little wife. Oh, Tom had so many grand plans for the two of us."

"What did you do?"

"I walked out of the restaurant. Tom followed me. Told me that I couldn't blow his chance. You see…he only got the job with Luther if *I* was his wife. Sort of a package deal. And he really wanted that job."

The sonofabitch should have wanted you.

"I told him the man I loved would never make a deal with Luther Bates. Not for anything. He laughed and said that I didn't understand just how much money was involved. We could have everything. The world would be ours." Her voice turned distant. "But I didn't want the world Luther Bates offered. Not after all the things he'd done. I mean, was I seriously supposed to smile and act like my father was an adoring man and not a cold-blooded killer?"

The man I loved would never make a deal with Luther Bates.

"Zoe…" This shit was going to be brutal. "There is something you need to know."

"Sorry." She stepped away from him. "I didn't mean to get all heavy on you like that. But I was serious—you do make me happy, Victor. For once, I don't have to worry that you're trying to get in on my father's good side."

No, I'm just trying to take down the bastard, by using you. Victor felt like absolute shit. "Listen, Zoe—"

And then he heard it. A tap on the door. His head whipped toward the sound. Someone was on the other side of that motel room door. *Not* one of his team members, not at that time of the night. Victor didn't waste any time second guessing himself. Didn't try to call out a warning. He just grabbed Zoe and they slammed down onto the floor...

Right before bullets blasted through the door.

CHAPTER FIVE

The bullets hadn't made a sound—there had been no thunder, no explosions that blasted like fireworks.

One moment, Zoe had been realizing that she'd just done a *serious* overshare with Victor, and in the next instant Victor had tackled her to the floor…and bullets had started flying.

The only sounds she could hear were the crack of the wood as the bullets flew through the thin motel door and the shatter of glass as they blasted out the window on the other side of that little room.

"Don't move," Victor whispered into her ear.

She needed to move. They needed to move. They needed to get the hell out of there.

The shooter was obviously using a silencer again, but…somebody must have heard the glass breaking, right? Didn't that mean someone would be rushing to their rescue? And, dammit, Victor had said this place was safe!

He reached around her, moving his hand toward the small, bedside table. She squinted hard in the dark and realized that he'd just grabbed his gun. Zoe couldn't even remember the guy leaving the gun on that table, but she had been, uh, a little busy before they'd gone to bed. She'd also closed her eyes and faked sleep during his stripping adventure, so maybe she'd missed the gun part entirely.

He eased the weapon off the nightstand.

The guy at the door had stopped firing.

Why isn't someone coming to help us?

"There's no point in dying for her, is there, Special Agent?" It was a man's voice. No accent. Clear and calm and almost friendly.

Victor's gun was inches from her face. His body was still on top of hers, his legs between hers. He was wearing his jeans and nothing else. Since she was only clad in her underwear and bra, the pose was pretty damn intimate…or it would have been, if they hadn't been so close to dying.

"I'm not here to kill you, Special Agent," the man continued. "So you can just turn away and not get hurt. She's the one I need."

"*Too fucking bad,*" Victor whispered.

"And I'm afraid…" The door gave a long, low groan as it opened. What had he done? Shot the flimsy lock? "I'm afraid that I can't leave without her—"

Victor had his gun aimed at the door and when he heard that door groan once more, he fired.

The thunder of his gunfire had her ears hurting. He shot once, twice.

The guy in the doorway cried out — a pain-filled sound — but he fired back. Victor grunted, and he shoved off Zoe. His gun blasted once again.

Then —

A long, low moan drifted across the room. Zoe was still on the floor, afraid to move, afraid to make herself any more of a target.

"No damn way were you getting her," Victor said.

Then the lights flashed on.

Zoe blinked against that too-bright light. Then her gaze jerked toward the doorway — and Victor.

He still had his gun in his hand. His muscles were locked, tense and powerful, as he stood over his prey. His *bleeding* prey. Because the guy on the floor had been hit, and blood was already soaking his shirt. The guy's skin was ashen, and his body shuddered.

A gun was near the injured man's right hand. But, the guy's hand? It was currently crushed beneath Victor's foot.

Zoe scrambled forward and grabbed that gun. It was slick in her hands. No, her *hands* were slick with sweat. And the gun was freaking huge, mostly because of the big silencer on it.

"You're dying." Victor's words were flat. "You know you're fucking dead. No way you live long enough for help to get here."

Ice coated Zoe's skin. All that blood… *Victor's right.*

"So do one good thing with your life," Victor continued, voice grating. "Tell me who hired you. Tell me who sent you after her."

The man's gaze slid toward Zoe. A blue gaze, filled with pain. Fury. Fear. "You…you won't live long…either…"

"Who the fuck hired you?" Victor snarled.

"He won't…save y-you…" The guy was spitting blood as he talked. "Others…k-keep c-coming…" His body jerked but he kept smiling.

Zoe's chin lifted. "Yes, maybe someone else will come after me. But you know what? I'm not the one dying tonight. *You* are."

And the fear grew in his eyes. This man—this hitman had taken so many lives—and now he was afraid of dying.

"How do you think they all felt?" Zoe asked him. "Your victims? Do you think they were as scared as you are?"

His smiled faded. That fear was so bright and strong and when the last breath wheezed from his lungs…

The fear was still in his eyes.

Oh, God. He just died right in front of me. Her hands were shaking so badly, jerking and trembling as she checked for a pulse that wasn't there.

Victor's fingers closed over hers. "Let me take the gun."

Her gaze snapped away from the dead man as she focused on Victor's face.

"I don't want you to accidentally fire." He pulled the gun from her. "No more wounds tonight."

That was when she realized — "You're bleeding!" Blood was streaming down his arm.

And a dead hitman is at our feet. How is this my life?

"Flesh wound." Victor shrugged it off, like a bullet wound was totally nothing to him, being the super special agent that he was. *Bullshit. A bullet wound is a bullet wound!* "We need to get out of here."

She shook her head.

"This place is seriously compromised. With the bounty on your head, another hitman could show any second." He pushed her toward the bed, *away* from the body. "I'll call Russell and he can get a clean-up crew out here."

A clean-up crew? "Luther used the same kind of crew." She wrapped her arms around her stomach. Held tight. "Heard him call for them before…"

His eyes narrowed on her. "You *heard* your father call for a team to clean up after a murder?"

Zoe…be careful. "I'm sure the FBI's team is much different. You're not just going to make the body disappear, right?" She hurried toward the bed. She dressed as quickly as she could and tried extra hard *not* to glance back at the dead man. She didn't know him. He was a complete stranger to her. A stranger who'd been ready to kill her for money.

Most people will sell out their own families for that much money.

"What body did your father make vanish?"

She was dressed. So was Victor. She hadn't even realized he was putting on the rest of his clothes and his shoes. When she looked at his arm, she saw that the blood was soaking the sleeve of his shirt. "Luther is in jail for killing four of his associates." She felt numb. "Why does another body matter to you now? It's not like he's getting out."

His jaw locked as he turned away from her. "Don't be too sure," he muttered.

"What?"

But he'd bent near the body. His hands went to the guy's pockets.

"Victor! What are you doing?"

Victor lifted his hand, holding a key ring. "I thought I got the tracker off our ride. Maybe there was another one on the SUV that I didn't see. Or maybe he followed Russell and Lauren here—I don't know how he found us, but I'm not taking chances." He gave a grim nod. "What I *am* taking…is his ride. No one should be able to follow us in that."

He'd put his holster back on and tucked his gun inside. The dead man's gun—that was on the bedside table now. Victor pulled out his phone and put it to his ear.

Zoe's gaze kept sliding to that dead man. *Not my first body. With Luther as my father, how could it be?* But it never got easier. Even knowing that the guy had wanted her dead…

Never any easier.

"Russell?" Victor spoke into his phone. "Yeah, yeah, get back to the motel and bring a crew with you." A slight pause. "No, I found the bastard. Or rather, he found us. He's here, and I'll need you to take care of him."

She shivered.

"No, you won't be able to question him. You can't question the dead. He came in, gun blazing. I had to return fire."

Because he'd been saving her life. The hitman had given Victor the option of walking away. Of saving himself.

Instead, he killed…for me.

"I'm getting Zoe out of here. I'll call again when we're secure. You run the guy's prints, check his DNA. Find out everything you can about him, got it? I'll check in as soon as I can."

He pushed the phone into the pocket of his jacket. Then he was reaching for her again. They stepped over the body. *God, it feels wrong to just leave him!* And a moment later, they were out in the cold night air.

"No one came," Zoe whispered. "Someone must've heard the glass shatter — or the blast of your gun." He'd had no silencer on his weapon. "But no one came to help."

"That's because this isn't the helping kind of place." He headed straight for the darkest part of the lot — and, sure enough, a motorcycle waited there. He put the key in the bike and had it growling to life. "When folks hear noises like that here, they hunker down. Helping is the last thing on their minds." He straddled the bike and offered her his hand.

"We are going to freeze our asses off on that thing," Zoe warned him.

He smiled. "Don't worry. I won't keep us on the roads too long. Priority one is getting you away from the scene. Priority two is making sure I use a ride that *can't* be traced tonight."

She climbed on behind him. He gave her the helmet to wear.

"Hold tight," Victor told her.

She locked her arms around him. "Where are we heading?"

"I made a deal with you, didn't I? You want to find your friend Michelle, and since we both know she was last seen in Vegas...Sin City, here we come."

"But that's like...twenty hours away." They were *not* riding the motorcycle that whole way, were they? They'd be frozen long before they made it.

"Don't worry. I have a friend who I can call to help us out."

And the motorcycle zoomed out of that parking lot. *A dead man's bike.* She held Victor even tighter as the motorcycle's engine vibrated, shaking her whole body. The wind whipped against her, chilling her, but because she was so close to Victor, his warmth seeped into her. *He* took the brunt of the cold.

He was protecting her, again.

Victor Monroe.

The special agent she was starting to trust...

And a man she desperately needed.

***

Russell gave a low whistle when he walked into the motel room and saw the body on the floor. "Guess he learned that Vic doesn't play around."

Lauren knelt near the body and put her hands on the man's throat. Russell thought it was pretty obvious that the guy was dead, but, hey if the new girl wanted to check…

She looked up at him.

He raised his brows. "Better get some gloves on," he advised. "You don't want to contaminate the scene." His gaze slid around the room. The glass in the window was broken. Some of the glass had rained down on the bed. A very rumpled bed.

Vic, I sure as hell hope you know what you're doing.

When he looked back at Lauren, her gaze was on the bed, too. And she was blushing.

New girl. He almost smiled.

"It's a good thing Agent Monroe was awake when the attack occurred," Lauren said, clearing her throat. "Otherwise…"

"Otherwise Zoe Peters would be dead." Victor had always been a lucky bastard. "And he might be dead right along with her."

Instead…a mystery man lay on the floor. A guy who should've been able to get the drop in the middle of the night, but he hadn't. Because the hitman had made the mistake of going up against Victor.

"They're…involved, aren't they?" Lauren asked carefully.

Russell sighed. "Look, Lauren, just because you share a room with an asset…that doesn't mean you're fucking her."

She flinched. She really was going to have to leave that prudishness at the door if she wanted to make it as an agent.

"Is he...though? Fucking her?"

Russell wasn't about to touch that one. "Victor Monroe has a job to do. He'll do that job."

"Protecting Zoe..." She nodded.

That wasn't exactly the job. But Lauren wasn't on a higher clearance level, so Russell didn't answer her. He just paced closer to the body. His eyes narrowed. That guy...he looked familiar to him.

I've seen that face before...

He'd been involved with the Luther Bates investigation on and off for years. And he *knew* this guy—*you're connected to Luther.*

But...how?

Just where did this hit man fit into the mix?

***

Zoe and Victor took shelter at another small motel, one close to the airport. They stayed on the road for just over an hour, going far enough, fast enough, that Victor was sure no one was on their trail.

His fingers felt fucking numb by the time they walked into their little room—a room that was a damn sight nicer than the last place. He took off his coat, wincing a bit when his new wound protested the move.

"While you're taking things off, ditch your shirt, too," Zoe ordered.

He smiled at her. "Baby, I love that you're in the mood after everything's that happened —"

She growled at him and grabbed his hand. "Stop thinking you're God's gift and let me look at that wound, okay?"

"I told you, it's nothing."

"And I'm telling you…*I'm looking at that wound.*" She dragged him toward the little bathroom. He let her because, yeah, he probably needed to clean the graze. The last thing he wanted was some kind of infection setting in.

That ride on the bike had been colder than he anticipated. Was it December already? Hell. Time just kept pushing right past for him. The days were a blur of work. Missions that never ended. Deaths and murders and betrayals.

"You don't have to play the ice man with me." She was very slowly — and carefully — lifting up his shirt. The sleeve pulled on the wound, but he didn't flinch. He didn't want Zoe to think she was hurting him. "You killed a man tonight. I know…I know that has to make you feel…" But she broke off, biting her lip.

"How does it make me feel?" How was it supposed to make him feel?

She put his shirt down on the sink and turned on the faucet. In moments, she had a cloth covered in warm water and soap. She slid the cloth against his skin. Once more, she was very, very careful. His head cocked as he stared down at her. When was the last time someone had patched him up?

Other than, of course, an ER doctor. "I've had so much fucking worse, baby. I'm all right."

"You think I don't see the scars?" And the fingers of her left hand rose to trace over one of the thick, long scars that slid over his abdomen. "You've had too many wounds, Victor. You've come too close to death."

He shook his head even as her touch seemed to burn right through him. "I'm still standing."

"For how long? None of us will live forever, and when you face danger so much…" She stared at the cloth. At the wound on his arm — the newest wound. "If we'd still been in bed, still been sleeping, we could both be dead now."

"We're not."

"Because we got lucky." She washed off the cloth. Dried his arm. As she worked, she kept her gaze on his injury and she didn't look up into his eyes. "He didn't want to kill you, though. He was there for me. He even said you could walk away."

Victor's hand curled under her chin and he tipped her head back, forcing her to look up at him. "Did you think I was going to leave you?"

Her gaze was so deep. So green. "I wanted you to leave. I wanted you safe."

She actually thought he'd abandon her? "I would never leave you like that."

"Not even to save yourself? What is *wrong* with you?" Now she sounded angry. "Your life should come first. Not me, not—"

He leaned forward and kissed her. Not rough and hard. Not taking or demanding. Just...

A kiss.

Soft. Light.

Because he could be gentle, some of the fucking time.

"I would never leave you," he said again, whispering those words against her lips. He needed her to understand this. "I don't care how many hitmen come your way, I am going to be there. To get to you, they will have to go straight through me."

Her lashes lifted and tears gleamed in her eyes. "That's what scares me."

"Baby, haven't you noticed? It takes a lot to slow me down. Bullets, knife attacks...I don't get taken out easily."

Her gaze searched his. There were so many emotions in her green stare. "What are you doing to me?" Zoe finally said, her voice husky, breathless.

"I'm keeping you safe."

"No." She shook her head. "You are doing a whole lot more than that." She leaned onto her toes and pressed her mouth to his. "You're making me fall for you."

His heart jerked in his chest.

"That's so dangerous," Zoe told him right before she lightly nipped his lower lip. "More dangerous than you can imagine."

Hadn't she realized it yet? He liked danger. His hands slid to her waist, and he lifted her up, positioning her on the sink.

"Victor! No, your arm!"

"I don't even feel it." He kissed her. Not so gentle this time. Harder. Rougher. He was riding an adrenaline high from the night and that powerful surge just blended with his lust for her.

You're making me fall for you. Hadn't that been part of the plan? That stupid bullshit plan? Only…

Baby, you're getting under my skin.

He kissed his way down her neck. Her hands had fallen to grab onto the sink, holding it tightly. He wanted her holding *him* tightly, as if she'd never let go. He licked her. Sucked her skin. Felt the frantic beat of her pulse beneath his mouth.

"Victor…"

His eyes squeezed shut. Did she *know* that she sounded like pure sex? His every wet dream? That husky voice, that little moan that she gave…

"If you don't want this," Victor rasped. "Say no…now. Say it and I will walk away."

He'd walk right back out into the cold night air because he'd sure as hell need to cool off.

"I want this. I want you."

Those words were all he needed to hear.

His hand slid down her body. She kicked off her shoes, and they hit the floor with a little thud. He caught her jeans and her panties and pretty much just yanked the things off her.

Her breath panted out. Her eyes were bright with need. Her cheeks flushed.

"You are so beautiful." He meant that. He'd always thought she was beautiful.

His hands slid between her legs. There was something about watching his hand…seeing his fingers touching her, stroking her…*Zoe is mine.*

It was a primitive thought, unsettling. He'd never been primitive with other lovers. Sure, he liked rough, hard sex, but touching someone, feeling this strange link that went far past some civilized surface, that went straight to his core…

I don't know what the hell is happening to me.

She arched her back and gasped as his fingers stroked deeper. He wanted her to come, right there, with his fingers in her, with his gaze on her, with her body jerking at his touch.

He wanted to be in her, so fucking deep. He wanted her to know that she was his. He wanted her —

To think I belong to her.

"Victor! I'm so close —"

And his cock was about to burst in his jeans. But he didn't have a condom. Shit, *shit!* He kept stroking her. Her pleasure would be enough. He'd watch her, then he'd jerk off. Or, hell, just watching her might send him over the edge. His fingers slid over her clit and her hips pushed against his hand.

"In me, Victor! Come inside of me!" Her voice was demanding.

"Baby, I don't have another condom…" Just saying the words hurt. "This is for you. Just…you."

His thumb pushed on her clit and his fingers thrust into her. She came right then, gasping, her sex squeezing him tightly and she was so insanely gorgeous. Even more beautiful when pleasure swept over her face

Yes. He could watch her pleasure all night. Never get sick of it. She was moaning softly and her hands were on him, holding him close.

He kissed her. Savored her.

But then…

"Not just me, Victor." Her hands came between their bodies as she pushed him back. "I'm many things, but not a selfish lover." She unhooked his jeans. Slid down that zipper. Her fingers closed around his cock and she started stroking him. Long, sensual strokes.

His hands flew out and grabbed for the counter top. He looked over her shoulder. Saw his reflection in the mirror behind her. Hard face. Narrowed eyes. Clenched jaw.

"My turn..." She stroked hard. Pumped faster. He was so erect, Victor knew it wouldn't take long for him. The scent of her arousal — oh, hell, but it was driving him wild.

She pushed him again, just a bit more, just enough for her to slide off the sink. For her to ease to her knees before him.

He knew what she was about to do, and Victor almost came right then and there. "Zoe —"

She put her mouth on him, and his control splintered. The feel of her tongue, her lips...he was a goner. He held the counter as tightly as he could, and Victor erupted.

CHAPTER SIX

He could have said the desperate need he felt for Zoe was a byproduct of the mad adrenaline rush that had burned in his blood. Victor could have rationalized his desire for her by saying that he'd been in freaking turmoil after the shooting — that he'd been so frantic for her because he'd wanted a reassurance of life. That he'd wanted to wash his sins away.

But those lies would have been all bullshit.

Victor glanced toward the narrow bed. Zoe was sleeping. Dawn was coming, and the mess they were in…it was about to get a thousand times worse.

Because he hadn't been so desperate for her because of adrenaline or tangled emotions after the shooting or any other excuse that he wanted to throw out there. He'd been so wild…because he'd been with her. Because Zoe made him want and need like no other woman. When and where and why — did any of that matter?

He. Wanted. Her.

This case was becoming so twisted, with every moment that passed.

He took another long look at her, then he eased out of the motel room. He made sure to shut the door as soundlessly as possible. Then, not wanting to take the chance that Zoe might wake up and decide to use her glass technique to eavesdrop on him, he took a few quick steps away from the door.

A few moments later, he had his phone at his ear and —

"Victor." Russell answered immediately. "Are you safe?"

"Yes." He gazed at the deserted parking lot. "Tell me you ID'd the guy."

"You know you have to come in soon for a sit-down. This was a shooting, man. The paperwork alone —"

"Did you ID him?"

A long sigh came over the line. "The perp looked familiar to you, too, didn't he?"

Yeah, he fucking had.

"We're running his prints now and doing a DNA check with other cases. As soon as I have something, I'll let you know." Voices murmured in the background behind Russell. "I swear, I've seen his face before. Probably somewhere in all those files we have on Luther Bates."

Luther Bates. "I have a name you need to run for me." This part made him feel like absolute hell, but it had to be done. "When you're digging into Luther's files, look for an attorney…young guy, named Tom or Thomas."

"What's he done?" Russell asked.

Broke Zoe's heart. One of his many sins. "Let's just say I think he was pretty heavily involved in Luther's world, and I want to know where he is now."

"A lawyer…" Russell whistled. That was his thing. He tended to whistle when he was nervous or excited. "That would be the perfect person to turn against Luther. Lawyers always know where all the bodies are buried." He paused. "You know, a last name would be very helpful here."

"I don't have a last name for you, not yet. But I know the guy was in Vegas a few years ago, back when Zoe was twenty-one. He was involved with her. Asshole thought he was going to marry her."

Silence, then…"So I guess he knows all her secrets, too."

"No, he doesn't." The idea of someone else knowing Zoe's innermost secrets, her thoughts, her fears…*why does this piss me off so much?* "I want to know what the hell the guy is doing. Where he's been, what he's been up to…find out everything you can."

"It's working, huh?"

"What's working?"

"You're getting her to trust you. I knew if anyone could do it, it would be you. Has she told you any specifics yet about her father? Anything else we can use?"

"Yeah…" God, he was such a fucking asshole. "We need to take another hard look at her mother's death because I think Luther Bates may have killed her. And…Zoe was there."

"*What?*"

"Just get the case files, okay? I'm going off-grid for a while. When I touch down again, I'll be in contact once more."

"Uh, wait! Touch down? Touch—"

He ended the call. Not because he was an ass and enjoyed cutting off one of the few people that he called friend but…

Because he had to be very, very careful who he trusted, too. There had been a traitor in the FBI before, one who'd actually been working with Luther Bates. And someone *had* been recently leaking info about Zoe's whereabouts. So until this whole case was closed, Victor couldn't take any chances.

So he hadn't stayed on the line too long. He hadn't revealed too much.

Not even to Russell.

Victor headed back into the motel room. He locked the door behind him and stared down at Zoe's still form.

In sleep, her expression was peaceful. So relaxed. Almost innocent. Zoe had been hurt and betrayed so many times in her life. And now, she was starting to open up to him. She was giving herself so fully to him and he…

I am such an asshole.

He was supposed to destroy her.

***

"How exactly did you get access to a private jet?" Zoe leaned back in the leather seat, feeling all kinds of comfortable in her new jeans, sweater, and awesome boots. And all of that gear had been waiting for her…*on the freaking jet.* New clothes for her and new clothes for Victor. "Not that I'm complaining. I just didn't realize the FBI was quite this cash plush."

He sat across from her, and a half-smile hitched up his lips. "This flight isn't courtesy of the FBI."

"No?"

"It's from a…friend who owed me a favor or two."

"Nice friend." Though the way he'd hesitated and pretty much tripped all over the word *friend* told her that a whole lot more was going on with that particular acquaintance.

Victor glanced out of the window. "You heard of Drake Archer?"

She'd just lifted a glass of wine to her lips—seriously, there had been *wine* on the plane—and at that name, she nearly choked. "Of course! Who in Vegas doesn't know him?" The guy owned a huge portion of Sin City. "I danced for him."

Victor's head snapped back toward her. His eyes had gone all glittery.

"Um, Victor?"

"I didn't realize the two of you were so well acquainted."

She laughed. "I was a showgirl. Dancing was my thing. And trust me, I was pretty spectacular." She'd loved being on stage. Most people didn't realize just how much work went into those performances. She'd practiced endlessly. Each morning, she'd woken early, gone to her dance classes—she'd loved ballet and jazz so much. Then she'd headed for the actual rehearsals for her show. She'd pounded across that stage, tapping out her number again and again and again.

"I bet you were something to see."

Her gaze jumped to his face. She smiled at him. "When I was on stage, I became someone else. And not just because of the elaborate costumes…" Zoe laughed. "Though I confess, I liked those, too. I can rock some feathers."

"No doubt," he murmured.

"But it was different. The lights. The music. Out there, I was someone new."

"Not Luther's daughter."

Her gaze slid toward the window. She took another sip of the wine. "No, not his daughter. Luther was always East Coast. That was his area. I thought…in Vegas, I'd be safer. Out of his reach" She exhaled slowly. "But sometimes, it doesn't matter how far you go, does it?"

"Tell me more about the shows."

She let the memories sweep over her. Happy memories. When she'd been a showgirl, those had been some of the best days of her life. "It starts with boot camp."

"Boot camp?"

"Showgirl style. Doesn't matter how much dance you've had before, nothing else is quite like being a showgirl. So you start each show with at least a month of training. After all—you're not just dancing. You're dancing on heels, usually carrying twenty or thirty extra pounds just with your costume, and you have to walk up and down about a thousand steps…" Her heart kicked up as she remembered those days. "You go home exhausted, sure that you won't be able to move again, but the next morning…you wake, up, so ready to hear the applause from the crowd. It's addictive."

"And you…worked for Drake." A faint furrow appeared between his brows. "He didn't mention that to me."

"Not like he knew me personally." She waved that bit away. "Drake Archer has *people*. I was hired by one of them. I worked the show and was one of the best damn Bluebells there."

He blinked.

Her fingers tapped against her wine glass. "You have no idea what a Bluebell is, do you?"

"No clue."

Zoe laughed. She looked down at her chest, then back at him. "Two kinds of showgirls. Some do go topless...for certain roles. Others...like me...we usually had some kick-ass sparkly rhinestones that covered all our parts. Dancers like me are Bluebells."

His eyes had widened. "I will remember that."

"Good. See that you don't forget it." Her head cocked as she studied him and some of her happiness faded. Not surprising, really. Most of her happiness was fleeting these days. "Are you...all right?"

He just looked confused.

She glanced toward the front of the plane, then back at him. "After what happened last night...you didn't talk about it..."

"That's because I'm still getting used to the way I want you." His voice deepened. "I should have more control. I should keep my hands off you, but I can't."

Oh, wow. She sucked in a deep breath. Then another. "I was actually, um, not talking about us." She wet her lips. "I meant the shooting. The hitman." *Taking a life.*

A muscle jerked in his jaw. "Not anything to talk about there. It was kill or be killed. Only one choice to make."

He sounded so cold. "You don't have to be that way, with me." And she kept her gaze on him. "You don't have to shut me out like you do everyone else. You can talk to me. Tell me how you feel. How you *really* feel. Tell me your secrets—"

"Will you tell me yours?"

The question caught her off-guard.

"No, wait, forget it." He raked a hand through his hair. "You want to know how I *feel*?"

Maybe. Maybe not.

"I feel like the guy had it too easy at the end. He wanted to *kill* you, Zoe. He was hunting you like prey. He wasn't stopping. His only goal was to take your life, and shit, he almost succeeded. When I think of how close he came to killing you…" His hands grabbed the armrests on either side of his body and held tight. "I want to shoot him all over again."

That *wasn't* the response she'd expected.

He laughed, and the sound was bitter. "Wrong answer, huh? Not what an FBI agent is supposed to say, is it?"

"I don't know. I've never asked another FBI agent that question."

His stare raked over her. "You were supposed to be so much easier to handle."

Unease slithered through her. "You're…handling me now?"

He smiled at her. A smile that didn't quite reach his eyes. Nothing new there, he was always so guarded. Too guarded. "My job is to be your handler. Your protector."

"Why?"

His smile dimmed.

"When we first met…" Not a happy memory. Not even close. She'd been held captive in a basement, with a bomb strapped to her chest. Another of her father's enemies had been planning to kill her. "I asked you to just let me vanish. I wanted to disappear, not get sucked into the FBI's web."

"My boss had other plans."

"And just who is this boss of yours?"

"Assistant Director Percy Chase."

"Yes, okay, that name means nothing to me." But the fact that he was finally talking to her — actually sharing information about the FBI — that mattered. "Why didn't you just let me go? Why didn't the FBI let me disappear?" At first, she'd thought she was safe, but that illusion had been shattered fast.

The FBI had always been watching her.

Always.

"Your father…he's supposed to be working with us, did you know that?"

Now she was shocked. "Luther Bates never works with the cops."

"He does…if we have something he wants badly enough."

No, no, no. The plane jostled then, hitting some turbulence, and her heart shuddered.

"Do you know what Luther wants?" Victor asked her, voice completely devoid of emotion.

"Luther wants his freedom." This she knew. "He wants to be back out on the streets and back in full power."

Victor nodded, but he said, "Don't hold back, Zoe."

"He wants me." She said those words in a quick rush, like they were a dark secret that no one else should hear.

"He does. You're his family, Zoe. He wants to make sure that you're protected. The FBI pulled you back in…because that's part of the deal we have with him."

"I don't think I want to hear anymore." She didn't. Not another word about her bastard of a father. She'd already figured this out, anyway. After all, she'd known there *must* have been a reason she had FBI guards. Why they were trying to keep her alive. Why—

"As long as you stay alive. Luther has promised that he'll cooperate with us. And he has been…giving up some bits and pieces about his empire. Telling us about his enemies. Their organizations. Helping us to make drug busts. To stop cartels. To find shipments of weapons." He gave a grim shake of his head. "Luther may be behind bars, but he still knows *exactly* what is happening on the streets."

"Because he still has control." Another jostle of the plane had her whole body tensing.

Victor started to speak. She saw his lips part, but then he stopped.

"What?" Zoe asked.

No answer.

"Victor…"

He unhooked his seat belt and came to sit beside her. "You're afraid."

The plane jerked again. "The plane won't stop bouncing." And to think, she'd been so impressed by the fancy jet. *Not anymore.*

He checked her seat belt, then twined her fingers with his. "You're safe."

Sharp laughter escaped her. "You tell me that a lot, but…" She squeezed his hand. "I don't always believe you," she confessed.

"I know." He lifted their twined fingers and kissed her knuckles. "I'm working on that issue."

He was so confusing. "You want me to feel safe?" Zoe asked him. "Then distract me. Tell me something. Tell me about *you*." Because she'd been the one doing all the talking. All the sharing.

"Fine. You ask me anything—anything at all—and I'll answer you honestly."

Okay. "Why did you join the FBI?"

Silence.

"Victor…"

"Because I would have made too good of a criminal."

What?

The plane bounced, she squeezed his hand harder, and her attention stayed on him.

"I grew up hard," Victor told her. His eyes seemed to turn darker with whatever memories he experienced. "I was on the street most days, and I spent plenty of nights literally fighting to survive."

At those words, her gaze dipped to their joined hands. She looked at his knuckles—really looked at them—and saw the faint scars that lined his hands.

"The fights weren't exactly sanctioned. You stayed in the ring until your opponent couldn't move or until you were the one who got dragged out."

That couldn't be Victor's life. He was…
That isn't him.

"I was barely skirting the law most days. Going down a path I *shouldn't* take. A path that was too easy, but I fucking didn't want to end up a criminal. I had a choice. I figured, maybe if I was so good at the criminal life…if I could think like them…maybe I could stop some of them."

Her breath left her in a quick rush. "So you risk your life every day —"

"Because I've seen firsthand just how many lives are destroyed by monsters. By men like…"

But he stopped.

She didn't. "Men like my father."

His head inclined toward her.

"Thank you for telling me," she whispered.

Once more, he raised their joined hands to his mouth and pressed a quick kiss to her knuckles.

It took her a few moments to realize… "No more turbulence."

"No. It's stopped."

But he didn't let her hand go.

And she didn't mind.

***

When the plane touched down in Vegas, Victor escorted Zoe out of the airport, and he found a sleek limo waiting for them.

His brows rose at the sight. Drake Archer was leaning against the back of that limo, dressed in a high-priced suit and wearing dark glasses. His blond hair was tousled, and a smirk rested on his face.

Drake smirked well.

He was a tough sonofabitch. Smart. Dangerous. Victor hadn't much cared for him when they first met, mostly because Drake had been too interested in—

One of the limo's back doors opened. "You think you can come to Vegas, use my husband's jet and *not* call me?" Jasmine Archer demanded, her red hair shone under the airport lights.

Jasmine. Jazz. The closest thing to a sister he'd ever had.

Beside Victor, Zoe had stiffened. She probably wondered what in the hell was happening. He should explain things to her. Only—

Jasmine rushed forward and gave him a hug. "Seriously, I should kick your ass," she muttered. "Coming to *our* town and not calling me. Trying to leave me out of the fun."

"It's not about fun." Dammit. She wasn't working with the FBI any longer. He was trying to keep her safe. "I'm working a case."

Jasmine eased back. She glanced from him to Zoe, then back to him. Speculation glinted in her eyes. Then she smiled at Zoe, flashing the dimples that always made her look deceptively innocent, and offered her hand. "Hello, there. I'm Jasmine, Drake's wife."

Shock flashed across Zoe's face. "I'm Zoe. Zoe—"

"She's just Zoe," Victor interrupted, knowing that he sounded too gruff, but he'd busted ass to give Jasmine a *safe* life. The last thing he wanted was for her to get too involved in the mess that was his case with Luther Bates. He tossed a glare at Drake. "I asked for the plane. The plane and a low profile."

Drake shrugged.

Zoe was still shaking Jasmine's hand.

Victor tugged her free of the other woman and pretty much pushed them all into the limo. Just standing around outside wasn't the safest plan ever. When the door shut behind them and the driver started the car a few moments later, Victor tossed a hard glare at Drake. "Is it so much to ask that you keep Jasmine safe?"

Drake's eyes turned to slits. "You know I'd give my life to protect her."

Actually, yeah, the guy almost had done that very thing.

Jasmine cleared her throat. "We don't have secrets, Vic." Her fingers twined with Drake's. "It's kind of our thing."

He could feel his cheeks flushing. Only Jasmine could do that to him. He'd met her so many years ago. When he'd been a different person. When *she* had been.

He, Jasmine, and their third damn Musketeer, Saxon Black. They should never have formed that weird ass family unit. They should have *hated* each other. Or at least, he and Saxon should have.

He and Saxon had been fighters, in a match that had been far from legal. They'd been kids, too big and too strong. Rough teens. Their job had been to pound each other until only one guy was left standing. Too bad he and Saxon had both been very good at giving punches — and taking them.

Their fight had gone on too long. And in the end, they'd both still been on their feet, staggering.

Everyone else had left. He and Saxon had been about to collapse, then Jasmine had appeared. She'd patched them up. Kept them both alive.

And the three of them…*for a long time, it was the three of us against the world.*

But Jasmine was with Drake now. And Saxon…the guy had cut ties with the FBI and moved out to California…where he was currently settled with his new wife.

A wife who had some very, very personal ties to Zoe. *I can't tell her about those ties.*

More secrets. More lies. *Because that's our thing.*

Victor's gaze darted around that darkened limo. Traveling via the private jet had definitely saved them a whole lot of time. Now the big goal would be to keep Zoe out of the spotlight. He cleared his throat and said, "The fewer folks who know Zoe is in Vegas, the better it is for her."

"It's pretty easy to disappear in Sin City," Jasmine murmured. "I've certainly done that a time or two myself."

Zoe leaned forward, her shoulder sliding against Victor's arm. "That's why we're here, actually. One of my friends has disappeared. I came out to find her before but..." He felt her gaze land on him. "Someone cut that search sort."

"Because I was trying to save your sweet ass," he said, too aware that his voice had become a rough growl.

Drake gave a low laugh. "So...what? Something changed for you? You're not worried about her sweet ass any longer?"

Drake could be such a bastard. If the guy didn't make Jasmine so ridiculously happy...*I would totally kick his ass.*

"We have a deal," Zoe said, her voice soft but carrying easily in the back of that limo. "Victor promised to help me find her."

Drake's fingers tapped against his knee. "I've had some experience with Victor and his...deals."

Was the guy still furious over their past? So Victor had lied to Drake. Betrayed him. *Let that shit go, man.*

"Victor helps you..." Drake mused. "But what does Victor get out of that deal? What's in it for him?"

I made her promise me anything. Would she admit that? No, no, Victor didn't think she'd reveal—

"That part is between us." Again, her voice was still soft. "But I know I can count on Victor. He hasn't let me down. In fact, he's the reason I'm still alive."

Jasmine was silent. A dangerous sign. Jazz was definitely *not* the silent type.

"Give me the name of the missing woman," Drake said. "I'll get my security team to start running down leads. If you're trying to stay out of the spotlight, let them do most of the recon work while you take refuge in my hotel. Trust me, you'll be safe there."

"No offense," Zoe said. "But trust isn't going to enter the equation for me."

"*I* trust him," Victor told her. And he did. It wasn't like he would have let the guy marry Jasmine otherwise. Drake Archer was ruthless, demanding, and dangerous, but he was also one of the good guys.

Semi-good, anyway.

"I trust him," Victor repeated, lowering his voice, wanting Zoe to know that he wasn't leading her into any kind of trap.

But I am. Sonofabitch, I am.

"Tell me the missing woman's name," Drake said.

Zoe hesitated. The car kept eating up the distance as it headed toward those bright Vegas lights. "Michelle," she finally said. "Michelle Lane."

CHAPTER SEVEN

Drake took them to a private entrance at the hotel. There were definite perks involved when you arrived with the hotel's owner. A private entrance, a private elevator. A quick trip to a reserved suite on the top floor that kept them away from prying eyes.

Drake opened the door to the suite and escorted Zoe inside. Victor started to follow them, but Jasmine reached out and grabbed his wrist, stopping him.

"What in the hell are you doing with Zoe Peters?"

Ah. Right. Figured that Jasmine would recognize her, even though he'd only let Zoe give her first name during the big introduction moment. Considering that Jazz had worked plenty of undercover assignments, she would have definitely been circulating with folks who knew Zoe…and her father, Luther Bates.

"I'm keeping her alive," he said, turning to stare down into her eyes.

"Bull. You're using her."

Now he was the one to turn his hand and grab her wrist. He pulled her away from the door. "What the hell?" His words were whispered. "Zoe might hear you!" Because *she* hadn't been whispering.

"Good. Maybe the woman needs to hear me." Jasmine jerked her hand free of him and glared — and no one could glare quite like her. Her eyes went all icy on him. "You do this. I've *seen* you do this crap in the field. You get all focused on the FBI and what it wants and you forget that real people are paying the price. Real people are getting hurt—"

"I'm helping her!"

She gave a hard shake of her head. "Victor, sell this story to someone who hasn't known you as long as I have. Let me guess…you told her that the two of you were a team? That you'd help her to find her missing friend?"

"Seriously, Jazz, lower your voice!" He threw a quick glance over his shoulder. Luckily, Drake still had Zoe somewhere in the back of that suite.

"In return for your help, what will you get? You think you'll get her to talk to her dad? Get some kind of family moment going so Luther Bates — Luther Fucking Killer Bates — will start playing friendly with the FBI?"

"He's already talking to us."

Her gaze widened. "Because you're protecting her."

Yeah. "He was *supposed* to keep cooperating. Supposed to turn on the other SOBs he'd worked with, but recently, he's started pulling back. There's some rumbles that he's working to get a new trial. The guy thinks he's going to get out."

Her breath expelled in a quick rush. "You suspect he's been stringing you along, huh? Just feeding you small fish as he bided his time."

That was the fear, yeah. "So we need something big on the guy. We need to get the power and *make* him cooperate."

Her attention shifted toward the suite. "I didn't think Zoe was supposed to be involved in her father's work."

"She *isn't.*" His immediate denial. And, yeah, maybe it was a hot denial.

Jasmine's brows shot up at his response.

"Zoe isn't a criminal. The FBI is *not* looking to bust her for anything." Hell, no. "But…but we believe she may know a bit more about his activities."

"Using her." She nodded, looking sad. "How many lies have you already told that poor woman?"

"You don't understand us."

"There is no 'us' here. There's you, doing your job, and then there's Zoe…falling for you."

His heartbeat quickened.

"Don't act as if you don't see it happening. It's in her eyes. In the way she watches you.

Touches you. Zoe doesn't realize that it's all just business for you, though. She doesn't understand that when you have what you want, you'll walk away."

Walk away...from Zoe?

"God, Vic, how can you be so cruel? How can you hurt her like that?"

He took a step back. "Hurting Zoe isn't part of my plan."

"That's the only way this ends. You get so caught up in the mission. In bringing down the bad guy. You don't see the collateral damage that you leave in your wake."

"I'm not hurting Zoe." He wasn't. He...didn't want to hurt her. He...*Zoe can't be hurt. I can make sure she's okay. I can —*

"Victor, I love you, but you are playing with too much fire on this one."

He glanced over his shoulder once more. Only Zoe was there now. Staring at him with — *fuck me,* with hurt in her eyes. Her gaze slid from him to Jasmine, then back.

No, no, no. Victor immediately hurried to Zoe's side. "I can explain."

But she backed up a step.

"It's okay." The words came from Drake. "She's his sister, just not one by blood." A mocking laugh slipped from him. "You think I'd let my wife's ex-lover borrow my jet? Hell, no." He strode toward a watchful Jasmine. "He's her family, and we all know…family can be a pain in the ass."

Zoe's lips curled in a weak smile. "You have no idea."

Yeah, she'd rather dominate in any My-Family-Is-The-Worst game.

"You two get some rest," Drake said, inclining his head toward them. "As soon as my team makes progress, I'll contact you right away." Then he and Jasmine were walking away. Their damn steps were even in perfect sync.

Victor glanced away from the couple and back at Zoe. Her gaze was shadowed. Before he could speak, she turned around and headed back into the suite. Victor hurriedly followed her. He locked the door and ditched his coat. Then he took a moment to take off his holster and put the gun on the entrance table. "Zoe…"

She stilled. She was near the big windows that looked out over the bright Vegas lights.

"I want you to be clear on this. If you…if you heard Jasmine saying she loves me—"

"I caught that part."

Okay. "She's like a sister to me. I don't have a real family. I mean, a blood family. Jasmine is *real*. She and Saxon Black—they are the only family I have."

She turned toward him. "I remember Saxon."

He sucked in a deep breath and knew that he had to tread very, very carefully here.

"Saxon," she repeated the name, as if tasting it. "He was the other man who came to my rescue when that damn bomb was strapped to me. The two of you were quite a team. Rushing to the rescue." She looked down at her hands. "Until he got shot."

Then he remembered that she'd put her hands on Saxon's chest, tried to stop that blood flow, tried to *save* him.

But Saxon had been rushed away from the scene. The guy had started a new life, with a new name.

"Did he make it? He...he did, right? Because the way you talk about him—"

"He's okay." Careful words.

"And...the woman who was with him?"

Shit. This was the part that was the hardest for him.

"The woman...Elizabeth. I-I knew who she was the minute I saw her. Or rather, the minute I learned her name."

His whole body went still. "What do you mean?"

"Elizabeth Ward. I heard my father raging about her before. Well, not her, but her mother. Her mother's name *definitely* came up in conversation."

"What did your dad say about her?"

"Oh, the usual. That she was a lying bitch who'd betrayed him. That she'd pay. That the whole family would pay." Her smile was sad. "You know Luther Bates. Betray him once, and every member of your family will be tortured and killed as payback."

Yeah, that was his MO. "So you…you knew that Luther ordered the hit on Elizabeth Ward and her family?" *What else do you know about Elizabeth?*

Like…*do you know that Elizabeth is actually your half-sister?* He was betting Zoe *didn't* know. Because even Luther Bates hadn't known that news, not until Victor had told the bastard.

"I found out after the fact…and by after, I mean when I was held prisoner and I was counting down the moments until the bomb exploded and I died." Her sad smile faded. "My captor was the one to tell me. I guess he thought I didn't fully understand just how much of a monster my dad was but…I knew."

Victor was afraid that if he spoke right then, he would slip up. Give away too much. He'd—

"My father destroyed that woman's family. I'm so sorry for what he did to her. And I…I hope Elizabeth is happy now. She was so in love with Saxon. I mean, that was obvious, just in the way she looked at him."

And he remembered Jasmine's words…

It's in her eyes. In the way she watches you. Touches you.

"Zoe…"

"Did she get a happy ending?" Zoe turned back toward the windows — and the city. "Even if she didn't, will you lie to me and say that she did? It would be nice to think that my father didn't destroy her completely. Good to imagine her out in the world, smiling and having some kind of amazing life."

He took a step toward her. Then another. He could see Zoe's reflection in the glass. "She got a happy ending. She and Saxon are damn deliriously happy." Saxon was like a new man.

"That's good." Her hand rose and pressed to the glass. "Nice to believe that some people can have that, you know?"

The woman was ripping out his heart. She didn't know Elizabeth was her half-sister, Victor was certain of that now. Zoe stood there, looking alone, too fragile, and so sad. She had no idea that she *wasn't* alone. She had family left in the world. Good family, not that twisted prick Luther Bates.

But I promised Luther I wouldn't tell anyone about Elizabeth. I fucking swore to keep her secret so she could stay safe.

Zoe had a giant bull's eye on her because the criminal world knew who she was to Luther. If anyone else found out about Elizabeth...

She'd be hunted, too.

The thick carpet swallowed his footsteps as he closed the last of the distance between them.

His reflection joined hers in the glass. He wanted to reach out, wrap his arms around her, and pull her close.

He also wanted to tell her the truth.

Don't trust me, baby. I am not worthy of you. You should kick my ass. You should —

"I envy you." Her words were so soft that he had to strain to hear them.

"Why?"

"Because you have people who care about you." She glanced back at him. "Michelle. Michelle Lane. She's been my only friend for so long. The only one who cared about me. You want to know why I'm risking so much to find her? That's why. Because she opened her heart to me. She helped me. She made me feel like a normal person for a while, and not just some pariah. Because being Luther's daughter, I've been a pariah pretty much all my life."

"We will find her."

Her eyes closed. "I understand." Her voice had gone even huskier.

"What? What do you understand?"

"How it all works." She exhaled softly and her eyes opened as she turned to fully face him. "I know that you want information from me. And when I promised you *anything* in return for finding Michelle, I meant that. You want more details about Luther? You want me to turn on him?" Her lower lip trembled. "I'll do it. I will.

Just help me to find my only friend. Help me to bring her back alive."

"She's not your only friend," he said.

A furrow appeared between her brows.

"I'm your fucking friend, too."

"No, you're not."

"Zoe—"

"You're my guard. You're the Special Agent in charge of my case. You're—"

He caught her hands. Pushed her back against the window and held her there, with her hands trapped on either side of her head. "This isn't just about the case. We're not just the case." First Jasmine had said that shit—and hearing it from her had been bad enough. But for Zoe to say it...*No. We are more.* His head lowered over hers. "We're lovers. That's what we are." His fingers had wrapped around her wrists. He held her captive right there, and as his mouth pressed to hers, Victor realized...

I never want to let her go.

He was so screwed.

***

Lauren McDaniel had only met FBI Assistant Director Percy Chase a few times—and each time, the guy had intimidated the hell out of her.

She stood in his office now, doing her best to look confident and poised, while the assistant director took turns glaring at her and Russell.

"Special Agent Monroe *killed* a man and then skipped town?" The assistant director's face had gone red, a very, very dark red. "What. The. Hell?"

"He believes that other hitmen are after Zoe," Russell said, his voice calm and easy, as if he wasn't even a little bit intimidated by the big boss.

I'm plenty intimidated. But she was doing her best to follow Russell's lead.

"Of course, they're after her! With two million dollars on her head, I'm tempted to kill the woman myself."

Her façade crumbled a bit at those words, and Lauren knew her gaze had widened.

The assistant director threw up his hands. The overhead light gleamed off his balding head. "It was a joke! Shit! Luther Bates can put most of the East Coast crime families out of business in one giant swoop—the guy just has to roll on them. Zoe is the key to him rolling. That means she's worth far more than two million dollars to me. She's worth everything." He sat down at his desk and huffed out a heavy breath. "Do we have a name for the dead man?"

Russell stepped forward and put a manila file down on the Percy's desk. "We do. Kyle

Lawrence. Guy was ex-military, an Army sniper, so his prints turned up in the system. Seems like Uncle Sam taught the guy some valuable skills…"

Percy flipped open the file. "Then he went freelance."

"Lawrence didn't usually go for up-close kills, but I'm guessing after he missed the first time with Zoe Peters, he realized he had to step up his game."

Percy grunted. "But his game ended." His gaze scanned the report. "So who is the power player here? Who's the one offering up the two million? Got to be one of Luther's former, uh, associates." He leaned back in his chair. "Luther should freaking realize if he cooperates with us, we can shut that asshole down before he offers up more money on Zoe's head."

Lauren cleared her throat. "Maybe…maybe he doesn't care what happens to Zoe. Or at least, he doesn't care as much as you think."

As soon as she spoke, Percy's gaze zeroed in on her.

But it was Russell who spoke next. "Lawrence looked familiar to me — me and Vic. So I did some digging. Once upon a time, the guy was hired muscle for Bates. But when Bates went to prison, Lawrence went off grid."

"One of Luther's ex-goons went after the guy's daughter?" Percy asked in disbelief. "What did the guy want—Luther to send the full force of his power raining down on him?"

"I think," Russell muttered, "he just wanted the two million. And he didn't care that he was screwing over his ex-boss to get the money."

Percy nodded, obviously buying that story.

I don't agree. Lauren straightened her shoulders—more than they were already straightened. "I did my research on Zoe Peters. Luther was hardly involved in her life at all. They've barely spoken since she became an adult. Why are you both so convinced that he's going to keep cooperating if we protect her?"

"I'm convinced," Percy said, his words clipped, "because Victor has an agreement with the guy."

Lauren bit her lip. "But what if Luther is just jerking him around? Using Agent Monroe? Using all of us?"

But Russell was shaking his head. "No. Not happening. No one uses Victor."

Perhaps, but... "We're not talking about some petty criminal. We're talking about a criminal mastermind." She inched closer to Percy. "He had plants at the FBI. Agents who were working with him. Is it really such a stretch to think that he could be manipulating us all now? Redirecting our attention?"

"The bastard has been meeting with a new lawyer in the last few months," Percy mumbled, rubbing his jaw. "We've known for a while that Luther thinks he's getting his ass out of prison. We've been watching for an escape attempt, but it looks like the guy must think he has some legal leg room to use in order to garner himself a new trial."

Russell stiffened. "You don't seriously think any judge in his right mind would ever let that guy out?"

Percy suddenly looked very, very weary. "I think Luther Bates has plenty of tricks left up his sleeve. That's why we need Victor to turn Zoe so badly. She *is* our last shot with him. Victor builds her trust, he gets her on our side and then we see just what damage she can really do to her father."

Lauren glanced between the two men. "So you don't think it's possible that Luther Bates could be the man who sent Lawrence to kill Zoe? You don't believe he could be the one who put out a hit on his daughter?" *Maybe he wanted to stop her from turning on him.*

Percy's gaze suddenly sharpened on her. "I think there are no limits to what Luther Bates will or will not do."

Okay, that was—

"And I think the FBI's main focus needs to be protecting Zoe. Turning Zoe. *Using her.* Before we lose her."

That sounded so…cold.

"We can't let Luther get ahead of us." He tapped his chin, considering. "Okay, okay...this is what I want. Find out all you can about Luther's new lawyer."

The lawyer? He didn't want them to try and discover whether or not Luther had taken out a hit on his own daughter?

But the assistant director had already turned away from her and glanced toward his computer. He typed quickly, opening a new screen as he said, "The fellow has some fancy ass name...Xavier Thomas Winters."

"Tom," Russell said, sounding a bit surprised.

"Yeah, well," Percy grumbled, "I sure hope the asshole goes by Tom. Xavier is—"

But Russell had already surged toward the assistant director's desk. "You said he was Luther's *new* lawyer, but Vic told me...he said that, a few years ago, a lawyer named Tom worked for Luther. The guy wanted Zoe to marry him."

Surprise rippled across Percy's face. Then he frowned at his computer scene. "That the same fucking guy?"

Russell glanced at Lauren. His face was grim. "I think we need to find out that shit, right now."

And I think we need to find out who the hell wants Zoe dead. Who is pulling all the strings? But she was supposed to follow orders. Wasn't that what a good agent did? So she said, "Any idea where this Xavier Winters is right now?"

Percy's jaw hardened. "Yeah...He's in Vegas."

CHAPTER EIGHT

The desire she felt for Victor always surprised Zoe. It should be wrong to want someone so much, to need another person so completely.

When Victor's lips touched hers, Zoe's heart seemed to stutter for a moment in her chest. She opened her mouth to him, kissed him back with quick eagerness.

She didn't like playing games. Didn't like pretending. Life was so short. What was the point in pretending?

She wanted Victor. Wanted him with a hot lust that she hadn't felt for others. Oh, sure, she'd been attracted to other men. She'd found pleasure with them. Tom had been a good lover but...

Victor is different. Everything is different with him.

When she'd seen him and Jasmine standing so close together, when Zoe had heard Jasmine say that she loved Victor...

I wanted to attack her. Not a normal reaction. She'd never felt jealousy before. Envy, yes, definitely. She'd envied the lives that others had. Envied their easy happiness.

But she'd never been jealous, not until she'd heard Jasmine speak so easily of love with Victor. Not until she'd seen…

Emotion, in his eyes. No shadows. No guarded expression. He cared for Jasmine. It was right there for me to see.

And Zoe had wanted Victor to look at her that way, too.

He licked her lower lip. His tongue thrust into her mouth as he tasted her. The glass was cold behind her back, and he was so incredibly hot. She could feel the hard length of his arousal pressed against her.

Her nipples were tight, aching. *Just from a kiss.*

His head lifted. His gleaming eyes met hers.

He still held her wrists captive. Still seemed to surround her with his heat and power. She stared at him, a thousand thoughts flying through her head.

Wrong man.

Wrong place.

Wrong life.

He was so wrong for her, in so many ways. But he was also the only man that had ever felt right. He'd saved her, again and again. Killed for her.

Was it any wonder that she was falling in love with him? "Victor…"

He kissed her again. A quick, hot, open-mouthed kiss.

This desire isn't natural. Maybe…maybe the attraction for him was due to some kind of weird hero issue that she had. When your father was a villain, maybe you rebelled against him and that rebellion took the form of attaching to the good guys.

Victor had saved her life — at least twice, maybe three times — but she'd started to lose count. Perhaps that was why she wanted him so much.

Or maybe…

He nibbled on her lower lip.

Maybe it's because he's…Victor.

And she really wanted to just give in to her need. To make love with him, right then, right there but… "Let me go."

He stiffened against her.

Then he instantly freed her hands and stepped back. "I'm sorry," he said, voice stilted. "I didn't mean —"

"I'm not staying here tonight."

"What?"

"I'm sure Drake has a really wonderful team of security agents. Top notch, truly. But Michelle is my friend. I know her. I know the places she'd go to hang out. The places she'd go to hide. *I* have to search for her. I can't just stay in this place, be in the lap of luxury with you, while she's out there…" It wouldn't be right. She'd come to Vegas before, looking for Michelle, but Zoe had been dragged back into hiding before she could find her friend.

No one will stop me this time.

"I want to stay with you." That was the absolute truth. "I want to make love to you and tell the rest of the world to just fuck off, but Michelle…"

His expression said he understood. "She isn't the rest of the world."

She's my friend. And I'm afraid too much time has already passed. Far too long. A woman shouldn't vanish so completely, but Michelle had.

"I can't stay here, with you, while she could be out there…" *Say it.* "Dead." Because that was what she feared the most. "I'll keep a low profile." It was the middle of the night — not like she was prancing around the city in the middle of broad daylight. "But I have to go out. I can't let more time pass."

He nodded. "Then I guess it's time for us to go." Victor turned and headed for the door. He put his holster back on, secured the weapon, and reached for his jacket.

She just stood there. "No arguments?"

"I don't go back on deals that I made. Remember that, will you?"

Zoe hurried toward him. "Victor, I need you to know—"

He turned toward her, but as soon as she stared into his eyes, her words tumbled to a halt.

"What? What is it you want me to know?"

Zoe swallowed. "Thank you."

"For what?" He smiled. She loved his smile. She just wished she could see it more often.

"For being a man I can trust."

His smile faltered. "No, Zoe…"

She leaned onto her toes and pressed a quick kiss to his cheek. "Thank you," she said again.

Before he could reply, his phone started ringing. She felt the vibration against her. Victor swore and reached into his jacket pocket. He pulled out the phone, then swore one more time when he saw the caller's name. But he put the phone to his ear and answered, saying, "Russell, shit, we haven't been in town long, but I was going to check in with you—" He turned away from her.

Her hands twisted together as she stood there, waiting.

"Who?" Victor barked. "Xavier what?"

Xavier. Her stomach knotted. That was a name she hadn't heard in a very long time. Though, he'd never really enjoyed going by that name. He'd preferred…

"Tom."

Her head snapped up and she found herself staring into Victor's gleaming gaze. As he looked directly at her, Victor said, "Xavier Thomas Winters."

She flinched.

"Yes," his voice had gone cold. "I do believe that's him."

Zoe wrapped her arms around her body.

"And the dead hitman? You got a name on him, too? You figure out why he was so familiar?"

Michelle needs you. Get the hell out of here.

She forced her legs to move as she hurried toward the door.

But Victor just moved to the side, blocking her path.

"Thanks for the intel, Russell. I'll call you later and we'll talk more." He shoved the phone back into his pocket. "Your former lover — the guy who wanted to marry you — "

"I already told you about Tom."

"You *didn't* tell me he was still working for Luther."

Shock ripped through her. "That's because I didn't think he was! The agreement — it was supposed to be a package deal. Luther told us that." Bitterness rose, threatening to choke her.

"Well, then I guess your father lied."

As if it would be the first time.

"Russell says that Luther's new lawyer — Xavier Thomas Winters — has been visiting him an awful lot in the last few months."

Chill bumps rose on her arms. "I need to start searching for Michelle." Once more, she tried to move around him, but he just side-stepped, going with her.

"He's here, Zoe."

She blinked.

"Russell said Tom is in town. He's in Vegas. *You're* in Vegas. Isn't that one hell of a coincidence?"

Uh, yes, it was. Only his voice was hard and his eyes were cold. "What are you implying?"

"We'd taken you off the radar. We'd made you vanish. Then you convince me to break all the rules and get you back to Vegas. When *he's* here. A guy working with your father and —"

Wild laughter escaped her. "You think I'm setting you up? That this is some — some what? Some game? Some big ruse so that I could come out of hiding and go away with Tom?"

His eyes glittered.

"No!" She was pretty much yelling and she didn't care. "No, I'm not lying to you. I'm not betraying you. I haven't seen Tom since that day — the day I said he could have me and we could walk away from Luther, together. *He could have me.* But I wasn't enough." Humiliation burned through her at that stark confession. "He didn't want me. He just wanted power." She swiped her hand over her cheek. "Now get the hell out of my way. Because I have a job to do."

She didn't think he was moving. She was about to push that guy out of her way—

"There's something else you need to know." He hesitated. *Still in my way.* "The hitman has been ID'd. He's a guy who used to be on your father's payroll."

"What?"

"Russell thinks the fellow went freelance after Bates went to prison."

Okay, yes, she could buy that.

"Or…or maybe…"

She stiffened. *Maybe he's still working for Luther?* "You said Luther wanted you to keep me safe. So it doesn't make any sense that he'd hire someone to kill me." Zoe shook her head. "It wouldn't be the first time someone turned on Luther. Not the first time, not the last."

"Zoe—"

"*Michelle.*" She nearly shouted the name at him. "She's what I have to focus on right now, got it?" She already felt like she was ripping apart. "I can't—I can't do anything else. I can't think about Luther or the hitman or *anything else*. I need to find her. Now either get out of my way or come with me."

Without another word, Victor turned away from her. He opened the door. Held that door while she marched out.

He didn't speak to her again, not until they were inside the elevator and heading down to the lobby. Then Victor said, "Tom was a damn fool."

Her breath left her in a fast gasp.

"Any man in his right mind would have chosen you...*You are enough. You are more than enough.*" His hands fisted at his sides. "He should have known you were everything."

The ache in her chest eased, just a little bit. The ache eased, but the fear—her new companion—stayed.

***

Getting into Michelle Lane's apartment wasn't hard. It also wasn't exactly a legal entrance or search, but Victor figured desperate times...

Desperate times mean I break more rules for Zoe.

When they'd been in Drake's hotel and tears had glistened in Zoe's eyes as she'd said that she hadn't been enough, when he'd heard the pain in her voice...*I wanted to hunt down Xavier Thomas Winters and beat the guy's ass.*

Only Victor was supposed to be the good guy. The guy who didn't use his fists to get some much needed vengeance for Zoe.

"It looks as if she hasn't been here in weeks," Zoe said, spinning around in the middle of the little den. "There's dust everywhere. Michelle is a neat freak. Like, obsessively neat. No way would she be letting the place get this way if she'd been here recently."

Not a surprise. They'd already known the woman had vanished from the radar, but Victor had wanted to search Michelle's place just in case there might have been some clues there. Signs of a struggle. Notes about travel plans...clothes that were packed indicating she'd left *willingly.*

But...

There's nothing. No broken furniture. No overturned chairs. All of her clothes are still hanging in the closet, precisely in place.

In fact, other than the dust, the whole place was...perfect. Too perfect.

He slowly turned around, studying all the walls. No photos. He opened a few drawers. Some were bare. Some had only the fewest of items — a screwdriver, matches. "Your friend..." he murmured. "She's not exactly the sentimental type, is she?"

"What do you mean?"

He shut the drawer he'd opened. "No family pics. No mementos from trips."

Zoe glanced at the walls. The empty walls. Then back at him. She rubbed her forehead. "I guess I never noticed. Is that…odd? That she doesn't have things like that?"

It was certainly interesting.

"I never had them," she murmured, rubbing her head a bit harder. "After my mom…died, it wasn't like I wanted to put up pictures of Luther. And I don't have any other family members."

Fuck, yeah, baby, you do. Guilt twisted in his gut.

"I guess I never noticed Michelle didn't have pictures because I didn't, either. Seemed normal to me." Her hand fell to her side. "She didn't talk about her family to me, either. She didn't ask me about mine and I didn't ask about hers. I was just—glad to not have to lie to someone new, I guess." She swallowed. "I should have asked. If I'd known more about her family, I could have contacted them. Could have found out if—"

"No next of kin was listed on her rental application."

"What?"

He rolled his shoulders back. "I did some digging a while back when you first went looking for her. I got access to her rental application." He'd pulled—or rather, yanked hard—on some strings he had. "She didn't have a next of kin listed. It seems that her parents died when she was younger."

"So we're the only ones looking for her?"

Maybe…

He headed toward the refrigerator. He opened it, expecting to have the scent of old milk hit him. Food gone bad. But—

The fridge was empty.

His head tilted. Michelle's clothes were still in her closet, her apartment—other than the dust—was completely clean. He shut the fridge door and strode toward her garbage can.

Empty. Very interesting. "She left willingly."

"What?" Zoe's voice rose, almost breaking. "How do you know that?"

He faced her. "Because your neat freak friend didn't want the food going bad in her fridge. She took it all out. Didn't just toss it in her garbage but probably walked it down to the dumpster."

Her gaze darted to the fridge. "Maybe someone else did that…maybe the person who took her—"

"Damn unlikely. The abductor would just be focused on cleaning up any obvious signs of a struggle. He wouldn't give a shit about milk congealing in the fridge."

Excitement flashed on her face. "Michelle would care about that. It would drive her crazy."

"That's why she got rid of it. She knew she wasn't coming back here for a while. She ditched the food, emptied out her garbage, and just left the things that didn't matter."

Now Zoe surged toward him. "Her *clothes* are here. Are you really saying those don't matter?"

Actually…*maybe.*

"There are other places we need to visit." She nodded decisively. "A club off the strip. A quiet place with lots of dark corners. Michelle and I met up there plenty of times because it was a place where we could both vanish."

Victor was getting a real bad feeling about Michelle Lane. He'd sent a few agents to look for her before but the guys had turned up nothing, fast.

How do you vanish so completely?

Maybe the question wasn't how, though. Maybe it was…

Why?

Sometimes people vanished when they needed to hide their sins. In his line of work, he sure knew one hell of a lot about that.

***

Most tourists would miss Dice. The little club wasn't flashy like the places on the strip. It didn't have big, neon signs. It was tucked far away from the traffic, a small place with dark brick and tinted windows. A bouncer waited at the door, sitting on a bar stool, but he wasn't exactly stopping people from entering the place.

In fact, no one was lined up to get inside.

"You sure this is the right club?" Victor asked, as he scanned the street. To him, it sure didn't look like the kind of bar that would attract showgirls.

"I'm sure. Michelle…she even had a thing going on with the bartender. I want to talk to him. If anyone knows where she went, it should be him." She strode toward the bouncer. A big, muscled guy with tats on his shoulders. His dark hair was long, a little shaggy. The guy's hard gaze swept over her and he jerked his thumb inside.

Victor followed her. When the bouncer's gaze darted to him, assessing, the guy seemed to stiffen. For an instant, Victor hesitated. The bouncer's stare was too aware, too intense. It didn't go with his casual pose.

"Victor?" Zoe pushed.

Victor shoved a twenty at the bouncer and kept walking.

Inside, Dice was like a cave. Candlelight sputtered on a few of the tables. There was no music playing. Just silence. The occasional clink of glasses.

This scene is wrong. The place is wrong.

All of Victor's instincts were on high alert. Zoe had made her way up to the bar. She put her hands on the old, scratched surface. "Excuse me," she said.

The bartender turned around. The bartender was a male, had to be pushing seventy, with a grizzled jaw and a bald head.

"I'm looking for Roy. Is he working tonight?"

The bartender's face hardened. "Don't know any Roy."

"Uh, yeah, you do," she replied, leaning toward him. "I've seen you…here…with him. He worked the bar."

The bartender's stare slid to Victor. "Better get your girl out of here. She's confused."

"She is *not* confused," Zoe snapped right back at him. "I've been in here at least a dozen times with Michelle! She was dating Roy. Roy who worked here, with you. He's a big, blond guy. She's a tall, slim, gorgeous African American woman with—"

"Get her out." The bartender pointed at Victor. "And don't let her come asking about Roy again. Roy didn't work here. He was never here." He turned away. Went back to clinking the glasses behind the bar.

Zoe whirled around to face Victor. "What is happening here? *How* is this happening? First Michelle, now Roy. They can't both vanish."

Yeah, they could. He caught her hand in his. "We need to go."

"No! We need to find them—both of them! That was the deal, right? That was—"

"We're going." From the corner of Victor's eye, he'd just seen the bartender pull out his cell phone. The guy was talking fast now, whispering into that phone. Oh, hell, no, this scene wasn't good. "And we're going fast."

He made sure to position Zoe so that he could still easily reach for his gun. He was worried he might be needing it soon.

They hurried for the door. He could feel the rage practically pouring off Zoe. She thought he was letting her down. Going against their little plan.

Screw that. He was trying to keep her alive.

When they burst out of Dice, the bouncer was gone. "Another fucking bad sign."

"What's a bad sign?" Zoe whirled and put her hands on her hips as she glared at him. "What are you doing? You know that guy was lying to us! Let's go back in there and *make* him tell us what's happening—"

"We're getting out of here." Only there were no taxis nearby. "Come on."

"Victor—"

"Trust me. We have to go, now."

She kept glaring at him. He thought about picking her up and just hauling ass. The silence stretched too long. Time they *didn't* have to waste. He stepped toward her. *Sorry, baby, no choice here.*

"Fine," she gritted out before he reached for her. "But I am not happy about this crap."

Then they were both rushing away—pretty much running—and they hurried toward the narrow alleyway on the right. He could see the flow of traffic on the other side of that alley. Once they got through that little space, they'd burst out on one of the main roads. They'd get a taxi. They'd get their asses to a safer place, then he could figure out exactly what had just gone down in Dice.

He could —

A man appeared in the mouth of that alley, a guy wearing a big coat, gloves, and with a thick scarf wrapped around his neck. Even before that stranger lifted his right hand, Victor knew —

Gun.

He pushed Zoe to the side even as he threw his body down on top of hers. He heard the sharp blast of the gunfire, but he didn't feel the burn of a bullet hitting him — a good thing. He'd slammed hard into Zoe, and he hoped like hell that she was all right. He grabbed for his weapon, ready to return fire.

"Ow! Fuck! Sonofabitch — let me go!"

At that scream, Victor tensed even more. He risked a quick glance around the giant garbage bin near him — his current cover — and saw that the guy in the scarf was on the ground. *He* was the one doing the screaming. Mostly because the big, hulking bouncer they'd seen before — the guy with tats on the side of his neck who'd been slouched with such unconcern at Dice — that fellow had his foot on the shooter's neck. The bouncer also had a gun out and aimed at the fellow on the ground.

"Stop your screaming," the bouncer ordered. "Or *I'll* stop it."

The guy wisely clamped his lips shut.

Victor took aim at the bouncer.

The bouncer looked up at him. "See what twenty bucks can get you?" His voice was mocking. "I've got to be the cheapest protection you've ever bought."

Zoe was dead silent near Victor. He didn't risk looking at her. He was afraid to take his eyes off the two men.

Were they both his enemies?

Or…

"I'm a federal agent," Victor called out. "So you really want to lower your gun right now and let me take over this situation."

Laughter answered him. "Right. Like you think I didn't tag you for a fed the first time I saw you?"

"And you think I didn't tag *you*?" Victor threw back. "Like I'm going to walk into a place like Dice and not realize what the hell is going on."

"Victor…" Zoe's voice was hushed, barely reaching his ears. "What *is* going on?"

As he watched, the bouncer tucked the gun into the waistband of his jeans. He lifted his hands, holding them toward Victor, palms up, but he *did* keep his foot firmly planted at the back of the shooter's head.

"The bouncer is on our side," Victor said. But a heavy weight had settled onto his chest. Yes, he'd looked at the bouncer and hesitated. *Tagged you, too.*

"Our side?" She inched closer. "What the hell does that even mean? That he's not a hitman?"

"Not a hitman." Not if his suspicions were right. "A cop." Hell, and if the bouncer was a cop...if that whole place was a front, like he suspected...

Zoe is about to be in for even more betrayal.

CHAPTER NINE

The building was non-descript. Two-story, brick. The windows were covered. There was only one main entrance and…

The place was some kind of safe house for cops. *Cops.*

Zoe's palms were sweaty as she glanced around the little room. An interrogation room, if she guessed right. With *cops.* She'd never gotten along so well with them. In her general ranking of law enforcement personnel to avoid, well, cops were at the top of the list.

FBI Agents were immediately ranked second beneath them.

She sat in a slightly wobbly wooden chair. A square table was in front of her. One of the cops — the bouncer, actually — had poured her a glass of water and put in on the table.

The bouncer didn't look like a cop. He was far too dangerous for that. But he'd shown her his badge. Victor had called Russell and vetted the guy.

Cain Blair. Undercover cop extraordinaire.

Only he wasn't the only undercover cop in the room. Her gaze slid to the left.

Roy Duncan stood there, frowning. Michelle's Roy. Roy the missing bartender.

Only he wasn't missing any longer.

Because when Cain had delivered her and Victor to this place, Roy had been waiting there for them. Roy, with his sun-streaked blond hair and his icy blue gaze. Roy who'd pulled out his own badge and ID when Zoe had just stared at him in shock.

He was a cop. All along. Did Michelle know?

"I'll want the prisoner," Victor said. He wasn't sitting at the little table. He was pacing to the right and looking very much like some kind of angry predator.

"Sorry, not happening," Cain told him, sounding not the least bit apologetic. "The Vegas PD has dibs on him."

"He tried to shoot me!" Victor snarled.

"No, he tried to shoot her." Cain pointed at Zoe. "And really, she should have known better than to come back to this town again. Seriously, what do you have, lady, a death wish?"

Victor lunged toward him.

"Stop it!" Zoe leapt to her feet. "Just — *stop!*"

All eyes were suddenly on her.

Don't fall apart in front of them. Don't. "Dice is…what, exactly? Some kind of cop front?" That didn't sound right. There had to be another term for the joint but…

"It's a relay space," Victor told her. He was at her side now. Looking enraged. Looking strong. Looking as if he really wanted to rip someone apart. "When undercover cops need to deliver information, they head to spots like that one. Usually, they'll have a teammate there. Someone who can make sure the intel gets into the right hands, without the undercover agent blowing his cover."

His cover…

Her cover?

Don't fall apart. Zoe turned her attention to Roy. "I've been looking for Michelle," she said.

He met her gaze, unflinchingly. "I know."

"She…we had a system in place. A way for us to stay in touch." *Because she was my friend.* "I've been making my calls, but she isn't answering. Her place is empty and—" She stopped because his expression had altered, for just a moment. There had been the briefest of cracks in his visage.

Pity.

"No," Zoe whispered. But the truth was right there. All around her. All freaking around her.

"You weren't supposed to come back here," Roy said, shaking his head sadly. Then his gaze jumped to Victor. "Isn't it *your* job to keep her in protective custody?"

Her hands had fisted. Her nails bit into her palms. "Michelle was working undercover." *No, no, no.*

"Michelle was doing her job." Roy's lips thinned. "That's all I'll say about that."

She jumped at him, more than ready to swing hard because the pain was so strong inside of her. *Lie, lie, lie.* It was all a lie.

"Zoe!" Victor locked his arms around her and yanked her back against his chest. "Look, baby, I get it's tempting as hell, but I can't let you attack a cop."

Why not? It seemed like a pretty good idea.

"She vanished because she's on a new assignment," Victor said, his breath brushing near her ear. "That's why there's been no contact from her. Not because she was taken…"

Tears stung Zoe's eyes. *I thought…*She jerked free of Victor's hold and spun to confront him. "You knew, didn't you?"

A muscle flexed in his jaw.

"When we were in her apartment. When you saw her clothes were still there but the food wasn't…I-I saw your expression change, but I didn't realize…"

He swiped his hand over his jaw. "I worked undercover plenty of times, so I'd been to scenes like that before, yes. They were keeping the place ready, in case she had to resume the role again. But the food was ditched because —"

"Stop." She hated this little room. Hated the eyes on her. Hated the pity — pity that was even coming from Victor now. "Just stop." She didn't want to hear anymore.

Didn't want to hear…

Michelle wasn't my friend. She was using me, too. The way everyone does.

"She had a job to do." Cain's words were gruff. "We got word that a new player was moving into Vegas about a year ago and trying to take over. A guy with some powerful connections back East, connections tied to Luther Bates."

And there it was. *Every road to hell leads back to my father.* Her eyes were stinging. "And I'm supposed to know who the new bad guy is? *I was never involved in Luther's world.*" How many times could she say that? Scream that? Why wouldn't anyone ever listen?

"Getting close to you put Michelle in a prime position," Roy said. "She was able to…" His words trailed away.

"Able to do — what, exactly?" Zoe threw up her hands. "I had nothing to give her! I wasn't involved!"

"No, Zoe," Victor's voice was soft. "You were her ticket. Her *in.*"

She shook her head.

"These guys…" He waved to the cops. "They aren't after Luther Bates. They're after the guy here in Vegas. A guy Michelle needed to get close to. And in order to get close to him, she got close to you."

"That's not true."

But Victor kept talking. "If the man had ties with Luther, doesn't it stand to reason he wanted eyes on *you?* And Michelle was those eyes. She got close to you. Learned your secrets. And then she used them to gain this sonofabitch's confidence."

She played me. Zoe's gaze jerked back to Roy. Red stained his cheeks.

"I'm sorry," he said, sounding stilted and uncomfortable as hell. "You weren't supposed to find out."

"Because I wasn't supposed to come back?" Goosebumps were all over her. "I've been trying to contact her…again and again and…*OhmyGod.*" Her hand covered her mouth. *I did this.* Horrified, she backed up, hitting the table with her hip. "There was no new leak at the FBI. *I'm* the leak."

Victor's brows furrowed. "What are you talking about?"

"Back when you first pulled me out of that bus station in Kansas…you'd said that word had spread that I *wasn't* dead."

He nodded grimly. "I was trying to keep you safe."

Wasn't he always? "You'd spread the word that I was dead. You were trying to take all the targets off my back, but I kept trying to find

Michelle. I made the calls — I let her know I was alive. She didn't answer me, but that doesn't mean she didn't get the messages. And she used them." Her head hurt. "She turned the information over to this guy — whoever the hell he is — she turned me over to him, and that's why the hitmen keep coming after me. She offered me up as her ticket inside…"

"I'm sorry," Roy said again, miserably. Uselessly.

"Fuck sorry." She stalked for the door.

"You weren't supposed to come back!" Roy called after her. "I mean, hell, why come to Vegas? You knew this place was trouble! You — "

"Because I thought she needed me." Zoe stopped at the door and looked back at him, disgusted. "I thought that was what a real friend would do."

Cain swore.

"But I get the picture now." She yanked open the door. They were on the second floor, so Zoe hurried down the stairs, her steps echoing in the building.

"Zoe!" Victor was rushing after her. Victor. Poor Victor. She'd forced him to Vegas for nothing. Put him in the line of fire for *nothing*.

She hit the bottom of the stairway.

"Wait, Zoe!"

She didn't want to wait. She wanted to get the hell out of there so she could stop feeling like such a fool.

But he was fast. Damn him. His hands curled around her shoulders and he spun her back. "Stop."

"I don't want to stop. I want—"

"You didn't do anything wrong. You were a good fucking friend to her. You risked your life for her."

Her eyes burned. "We weren't friends." All along, Michelle had been using her. Not looking past the shadows that surrounded Zoe, not offering friendship in spite of Zoe's criminal world ties...

Footsteps thundered on the stairs. She looked up. Cain was rushing down toward her. No, she did not want to deal with him then. "Let's get out of here."

"Michelle went completely dark over a month ago."

Cain's words froze her.

"She *had* been working undercover, making her way up the ladder slowly but surely as she gained the trust of that group. She was sure she'd get to meet the boss soon enough, one-on-one, and that was what we'd been waiting for." He'd stopped on the second step from the bottom. Cain raked a hand through his hair. "This guy—he's so sneaky. Smart. He's some freaking shadowy puppet master who has plenty of fall guys to do his dirty work. Powerful guys who shouldn't be bowing down to him, but they are. The drugs have tripled on the streets and the weapons — they flow in like a freaking river."

Victor moved, positioning his body protectively in front of hers. Why? It wasn't as if Cain was going to attack her. He and his buddy Roy had already done their damage.

They all sold me out.

"Michelle used you," Cain said and his words were cold and brutal. "It was her job. She needed an in with the guy, and you were that in. We heard rumbles that he wanted you. Probably for payback against Luther Bates. Isn't that what everyone wants?" His gaze cut to Victor and his lips curled in a hard smile before he focused on Zoe once more. "*Everyone.* Being who you are, I'd think you'd have gotten used to that shit by now."

"Watch your fucking mouth," Victor warned him.

She put her hand on Victor's chest. "If I can't hit a cop, neither can you." Her chin lifted as she faced Cain. "You think I'm supposed to just smile and say… 'Okay. No harm, no foul. She was just doing her job?'" Beside her, Victor stiffened. "Screw that. She did do harm. I risked my life for her." For nothing.

"She went *dark*." Cain grabbed the wooden bannister. "You know what that means? It means no communication from her at all. It means we don't know if she's just in deep cover and can't contact us…or if she finally made face-to-face contact with the puppet master and he figured out that she was a cop."

Zoe didn't move.

"If he found out, she's dead." Cain eased down another step, his expression tight and angry. "Do you understand? She's —"

The second floor exploded. The boom was deafening, a roar that had her screaming even as the force of that blast picked Zoe up and tossed her through the air. And as she flew, as she screamed, she saw the flames rolling across the ceiling…

Oh, dear God…we're all dead.

CHAPTER TEN

"Two million fucking dollars…" Zoe heard the whisper distantly. It was almost…giddy.

She cracked open her eyes, but she just saw fire. Flames rolling. She coughed and her whole body ached. She was trapped — her legs and lower body were beneath some heavy chunks of wood. The stairs? The bannister?

Someone grabbed her wrist. Held tight. Tight enough that she thought the bone might break. And then she was being dragged by that punishing grip on her wrist, yanked out from beneath the chunks of wood. She tried to turn her head and see who'd grabbed her. "Vic…"

"He's dead. Not going to save you this time."

The voice was familiar, but it was hard to hear the male clearly because the flames were crackling and roaring. Heat lanced across her skin. Had he said…

Victor is dead?

"No." Her legs kicked out. He was dragging her by the right hand and her left flew up and yanked at his fingers. "Let me go!" Victor couldn't be dead. He was wrong. She'd heard wrong. Victor was fine. Victor was—

Lying a few feet away. His eyes were closed. His body still. Blood slid from a wound on his forehead. "*Victor!*"

A gun pressed to her cheek. "Stop your damn screaming." Her gaze jumped to the man who held that gun. Even before she saw his face, she knew who he was. His voice had clicked. He had clicked.

Roy was holding his gun on her. Roy was glaring at her. And Roy...

"I can kill you here, but I need you alive—if I'm going to get *her,* then I need you alive." He grunted. "Plus, there's talk of a freaking bonus...I like bonuses." He hauled Zoe to her feet, but kept the gun shoved against her cheek. "So play nicely, and I won't let this bullet blast through your pretty face right here and now."

Her gaze darted frantically around the burning building. The second floor was a wreck. Flames were rushing everywhere. Soon the bottom floor would be engulfed, too. She needed to get Victor out. *He's not dead. He's not.* The smoke was thickening around her, and her lungs hurt even as her eyes burned.

"Come on." Roy wrenched her toward the door.

No, no, if she left, Victor *would* die. Zoe couldn't let that happen.

She also didn't want a bullet blasting through her cheekbone. Roy hauled her toward the door. Another cop gone bad. Two million dollars could do that, though. Two million dollars could make a good man lose his soul.

Roy eased his grip on her when he went to open the front door. He had to be careful because the handle had to be freaking hot. He moved the gun away from her face. A few inches, that was all she needed. A few…

She slammed her elbow back into him, then she whirled around to face him. She kicked the gun out of his hand, then, for good measure, she kicked the bastard right in the face.

Blood flew from his nose.

That's right, asshole. This showgirl's legs aren't just for dancing. Hope you liked that freaking high kick.

Roy let out a guttural roar, but she was already rushing past him, going back into the flames and racing toward Victor. There were two boards on top of him. One of the boards had just started to burn. She shoved both boards out of the way, ignoring the quick flash of pain in her hands. "Victor!" Zoe grabbed his shirt front and dragged him away from the wall. There were too many flames there.

She inched to safety slowly with him. The guy was solid muscle. A dead weight. *Not dead.*

He's not dead. I can see his chest moving. He's all right.

Victor let out a long, low groan.

"It's okay," Zoe said, coughing on the smoke. "We're getting out."

"No, *he's* not." Roy's voice came from right behind her. His arms locked around her waist and he jerked her back. Then he lifted up his hand — he had another gun there, a smaller one. *A back-up gun? Don't cops always carry back-ups on them?* And he aimed that gun down at Victor's body. "He's dying right here."

"No!" The cry was torn from her. "I won't fight. I'll go with you, I swear. Just…don't shoot!" Because Victor wasn't trapped now. He was alive. He could get out. There was hope…

As long as he doesn't have a bullet in his chest.

The roof gave a long groan. Her gaze shot up. She saw only flames…so much fire.

"It's going to collapse! Shit, let's *go!*" Roy yelled.

He yanked her back and Zoe knew he was going to shoot. Because Roy was still aiming at Victor. That bastard was going to kill Victor!

"No!" She threw her whole body against him. The bullet went wide, missing Victor. *Missing him.*

She and Roy were on the floor. He had his gun pointed at her now.

"You are such a fucking bitch," he swore. "No wonder he wants you dead."

She smiled at him. "Maybe…but you're about to die, too."

The roof wasn't just groaning any longer. It seemed to be screaming. Fire rained down on them. Down, down…

Before the flames could hit them, Roy slammed his gun into the side of her head.

***

"You weigh…a freaking ton."

Victor's eyes opened at the low, grunting voice. He blinked a few times, trying to adjust his gaze to the darkness around him.

Darkness…

Flames?

"What the hell?" Victor lurched upright and found himself sitting on the pavement just outside of what looked like a freaking inferno.

"For the record," Cain muttered as he dropped down beside Victor, his breath heaving out. "I just saved your ass. That means you'll owe me. Big. And I will want payback."

Victor's gaze was on the burning building, not that cop asshole. A building he'd been inside…with Zoe. They'd been on the lower floor. An explosion had sent him hurtling across the room and—

Victor leapt to his feet and started running toward the flames.

"Stop that!" Cain shouted. "Stop that shit!" He tackled Victor.

They went down hard, rolling across the pavement. When the cop tried to hold Victor down, he drove his fist right at Cain's jaw. Cain flew back.

"Zoe is in there!" Victor bellowed when Cain tried to come at him again. "Get the fuck out of my way!"

"She's not!" Cain shook his head. "Listen to me. *Listen!* She's not in there! I saw Roy carrying her out. She's gone."

Gone? He swiped the dripping blood from his eyes even as he felt a dull throbbing near the top of his forehead. "What the hell do you mean?"

"I mean…" Cain gestured toward the fire. "Your lady isn't dead in there, okay? So calm down. She's alive." His hands fell and his face turned pensive. "Or she was…I think she was."

Victor grabbed him and shook the guy as hard as he could.

"He was carrying her out! Jesus! Stop! Or I will head butt you in your already bleeding head!"

Victor stopped, but only so he could glare at Cain. "You saw her being taken…and you didn't save her?" He wanted to rip the cop apart.

"I was busy dragging *your* ass out of the fire, you ungrateful bastard."

Victor shoved him away. "She was the priority! You save *her!*"

"Yeah, well, I'm getting she's the big fucking deal in your life and all…"

Victor threw a punch at him.

Cain dodged it, barely. "Would you stop that shit? I woke up, dragged my ass out from the pile of debris and *fire*, and I saw her trying to save *you*."

Victor stilled.

"She was dragging you. Doing her best to get you out of that place. Roy came up behind her. I was yelling but the flames were so loud neither one of them heard me."

The flames were a roar right then.

"I thought he was going to help her." Cain gave a grim shake of his head. "Then he grabbed her and he aimed his gun at *you*."

"He didn't shoot me," Victor said. His body ached, he had some burns, but no bullet holes.

"Because *she* made the bullet go wide. I was trying to find a way through the flames to help her, but then Roy slammed his gun into the side of her head."

Even though the fire was raging, Victor suddenly felt ice cold. "He's a dead man."

"He carried her out. I fought the flames and got *you out*." Cain turned around, glancing down the empty street. "He had split ass by the time I got out here. He took her. The guy betrayed us all. He was supposed to be on my team."

"I know that feeling." Victor pulled out his phone, but the thing had melted. "The bounty on her head is two million. Are you really that shocked that Roy would flip for that much money?"

"He was a good cop. I worked with him and Michelle for years. He's never been on the take before. He's been solid." Cain had pulled out his phone, too, only to reveal that it was smashed and nearly just as melted as Victor's.

Hell. "He's not solid any longer." Victor turned away from the fire and started walking down the street. "He's a soon to be dead man." *Roy has hurt her. He hurt my Zoe.* In the distance, sirens screamed. Someone had finally noticed the giant ball of flames shooting into the sky. About time. He looked down at his hands and saw that they were shaking. Rage beat in his blood, a dark fury that he'd never felt before.

And fueling that fury?

Fear.

I have to find her. She has to stay alive.

He kept walking down that street.

I need her.

***

She hurt.

It felt like a hammer had slammed into her head. Over and over again.

Zoe cracked open one eye. Then the other. She tried to move her body, but found she was tied, hand and foot, as she lay in a sagging bed. Frantic, she looked around her — saw the yellowed walls, the faded furniture. Broken blinds were over the lone window.

Another no-tell motel. Why do I keep winding up in these places?

Sunlight poured onto the bed — and her. Bright light that told her a whole lot of time had passed since the fire.

The door opened. A brown motel room door.

Zoe tried to speak when she saw Roy standing there, but a gag was in her mouth. A rough, nasty-tasting cloth that had been shoved into her mouth and tied behind her head — she could feel the knot pressing back there from the cloth.

With a long sigh, Roy shut the door. Then he leaned back against it, staring at her. "Stop looking at me like that," he said, actually sounding offended. "It's not like I'm a bad guy."

Victor. Had Victor gotten out of the fire? Frantic mumbles came from behind her gag.

"It's not even the two million that tempted me. I mean, I wouldn't turn you over just for that. I'm not a monster."

Victor! Where was Victor?

"It's for her." He took a few steps forward, moving closer to the bed. "I can't let Michelle die." His clothes were covered in ash. "I know I can get her back. If I offer you up, then he'll give Michelle back to me. He'll make the trade."

She shook her head.

"You're just not worth what she is, not to me."

He really loves Michelle. That part wasn't an act.

"So I'm getting her out, and if you have to die for that to happen, well, then it just fucking happens."

Her frantic mumbles sounded once more.

"I don't want to have to knock you out again," he said. "I don't like hurting women."

What?

"So just stay quiet until I can figure out how to work the trade, all right? The motel is deserted this time of day, anyway. You're not going to get some big rescue." He ran a hand over his face. "No one is coming for you. Let's just try to make this as painless as possible."

He was insane. She wasn't about to make her death easy.

"I'm going to shower." He turned away. "I smell like fire." Roy yanked his shirt over his head and tossed it on the floor. Then the guy just — left her. He went into the bathroom, shut the door, and the roar of water reached her ears.

Victor. I have to find Victor.

She waited just a moment, trying to give Roy time to actually get his sorry ass into the shower. *That way, he's less likely to hear what I'm about to do.* She counted in her head, and when she got to one hundred…Zoe rolled. She rolled her body right off that bed and she hit the floor with a hard thump.

Her gaze jerked toward the bathroom door. Still shut. The water was still pounding down. Good sign.

She twisted her body, contorting easily. Did Roy have any idea how many dance and gymnastics classes that she'd taken over the years? It was all too easy for her to drag her bound hands under her ass and then around her now up-drawn knees. Soon her bound hands were yanking at the gag, getting that thing out of her mouth. She licked her lips, moved her swollen tongue, and then she tried to figure out her next move.

Cut the ropes. Find something to cut these damn ropes so I can get free.

Only no weapon was around. Then fine, screw it, she'd get out of there still bound. She was *not* going to be in that room when the guy came out of the bathroom. She had to take small, mincing steps with her feet bound, but Zoe slowly made her way to the door. One step. Another. Closer and closer.

But fear beat at her every moment. Not fear for herself. For Victor. Had he gotten out of the fire?

What if he hadn't? What if Victor had died in those flames? Died hours ago while she'd been knocked out and tied up in that bed? What if he was gone?

I'm not ready for that. I'm not ready to lose him.

Hell, no, she wasn't.

Zoe was almost at the door. Almost there.

The shower turned off.

Oh, God…

***

"Which fucking room is his?" Victor demanded as he slammed his fist down on the counter in front of the front desk clerk.

The guy flinched and his shaking fingers typed faster on the computer keyboard.

"Easy," Cain muttered.

Easy? There was nothing *easy* about the way he felt right now. The firefighters and the cops had finally gotten to them, and then they'd launched an all-points bulletin for Roy.

Only that shit hadn't been enough. And Victor hadn't wanted to just sit on his ass while Zoe was possibly being killed. So he'd called in favors and gotten more tech help.

Maybe Roy thought he was dead. Maybe the guy thought that both he and Cain had perished in the fire. That had probably been his plan. With both of them dead, who would be around to point the finger at Roy?

So the guy had left the scene, feeling all fucking confident. Confident enough that he'd been using his phone…

Your mistake. Your latest one, bastard.

Because one of Victor's favors involved getting a track on that phone. As soon as Roy used it, the signal had been triangulated. They'd found the jerk.

He was at the little motel on the outskirts of Vegas, and he'd *better* have Zoe with him. She'd better be alive. She'd—

"Room s-seven," the front desk clerk stuttered. "On the side of the motel, room seven—"

Victor was already running away. His gun was in his hand—a new gun, courtesy of the Vegas PD. His other weapon had been lost in the flames.

He rushed around the side of the building just as the door to room seven opened.

Wide green eyes stared at him in shock. Beautiful, unforgettable green eyes. *Zoe.*

"Victor…" She didn't make a sound, but he read his name on her lips.

And then…then she was jerked back. Her bound hands flew up into the air and the door slammed shut.

Oh, the hell, *no.*

***

"You tricky little bitch…" Roy had thrown her across the room, sending her into a heap near the foot of the bed. "Thought you'd just walk right out the door?" His back was to said door as he closed in on her. "I knew I should have knocked your ass out again."

She shook her head, tossing the hair out of her eyes. Then she smiled at him.

He stilled. "Why the hell are you doing that?"

"Because…"

The door burst open behind Roy and chunks of broken wood hurtled through the air.

"Victor got out of the fire," she finished.

"Get the hell away from her!" Victor bellowed.

Roy spun around. He didn't have a gun on him — the guy just had a towel wrapped around his hips. Water dripped down his body. He must have raced out of that shower when he'd heard the front door open. She'd known that sound had been too loud.

Cain ran in behind Victor, gasping. "So much for waiting on me…"

"Cain!" Roy staggered back a step. "You're okay! Good! Oh, shit, man, *she* started the fire. She tried to kill us all! I think she must be working with her father. I had to tie her up, to restrain her, I was about to call in backup when—"

"I saw you." Cain's glare was cold. Deadly. "I saw you attempt to shoot Special Agent Monroe, and I saw you hit Zoe before you took her out of that building."

Roy's body stiffened.

"So save the excuses," Cain blasted. "You're under arrest."

"I did it for Michelle!" Roy screamed. "If we want to ever see her again, we have to give that bastard what he wants—and that's Zoe! Not like she matters anyway. She—"

Victor attacked. He literally flew at Roy, and they slammed into the nearest wall. Roy tried to block Victor's blows, but that wasn't happening. Victor hit him again and again, and the sickening thud of his fists connecting with Roy's face had Zoe crying out.

"Stop, Victor! Stop!"

"*She matters.*"

Cain had to drag Victor off the smaller guy. Roy fell into a heap on the floor.

"She matters," Victor spat the words again, then he spun to face Zoe.

She stared at him a moment, seeing his rage. Such a hot, hard fury. His whole body was tense and danger emanated from him on waves. This wasn't some good guy. The controlled agent she knew was nowhere to be seen, but she wasn't afraid. Not of him.

Zoe lifted her bound hands toward him. "Victor, get me out of here."

He strode toward her. Yanked at the rope that bound her hands. Jerked it hard.

Uniformed cops spilled into the little room. One of them cuffed Roy. Another handed Victor a knife. He sliced through the ropes that bound her wrists. Pinpricks shot through her fingers. She hadn't even realized how tight the ropes were, not until then. Victor bent, then cut through the ropes that bound her feet. When the last rope broke, relief swept through her and she trembled.

Victor picked her up in his arms.

"No! I can walk!" Her tremble hadn't been about weakness. It had just been about her being grateful to be free.

But Victor didn't let her go. His hold tightened as he carried her out of that motel room. She looked back and saw a bruised and battered Roy — glaring after them. Glaring with the one eye that wasn't already swollen shut. Cain was reading the guy his rights, appearing absolutely enraged and disgusted, but still doing things by-the-book.

The sunlight was too bright outside. The air too cold.

Victor walked her toward a dark SUV. He opened the passenger side door and eased her inside. Then he just…stood there, his shoulders hunched and his head lowered.

Hesitantly, her hand rose and touched his chest. "Victor?"

"I thought you were dead." His voice was different. Colder. Raspier. "When I woke up, and the building was on fire and you weren't there…I thought you were dead."

"I was afraid *you* were dying in there," she whispered back. "I tried to get you out. I'm so sorry…"

His head snapped up. "You're sorry?"

Zoe nodded.

"You're sorry?"

Once more, slowly, she nodded. "I wanted to get you out. If he hadn't hit me with the gun, I would have—"

Victor backed away. He slammed the door shut. Paced. Paced some more. Tossed a glare her way.

Her hands twisted together. She rubbed at her bruised wrists.

Then he was marching around the SUV. Jumping inside the vehicle. He cranked it with a hard, angry twist of his hand. But then he stilled. "I'm the one who's sorry."

Zoe watched him.

"*I* let you down. I was supposed to keep you safe. Instead, I lost you."

"Victor…"

His head turned toward her, and the shield that was normally in place—the guard that stopped her from reading the emotions in his eyes—it was gone. Fury and pain and longing blazed at her. "I was scared."

"Me, too."

"I don't get scared. I get pissed. *That's* my way. But it was different with you. You're different. You made me different."

Was that good or bad? He made it sound bad.

"I couldn't find you fast enough. Couldn't get to you soon enough. And when I saw Roy…" He flexed his hands. "I wanted to rip him apart."

She reached out and touched his right hand. Her fingers slid across the faint scars on his knuckles. "I'm okay."

"*This* time. But what about next time? It has to stop." He gave a grim shake of his head. "It has to fucking stop." Then he shifted the vehicle and drove out of that lot with a squeal of tires.

CHAPTER ELEVEN

She's not dead. She's safe. Zoe's with me.

The elevator doors opened with a soft ding. Victor made sure that he stepped out first. They were back in Drake's hotel, back on what should have been a secure floor, but he wasn't taking any chances.

The area was empty, so he caught Zoe's hand and led her forward. She'd been silent during their trek back to the fancy hotel, a trek that had included a pit stop at the hospital so she could be checked out.

She'd glared during that process, muttering about just having bruises, but he'd wanted to be absolutely certain she was okay.

A concussion. The bastard gave her a concussion. And she's got black bands of bruises around her wrists and ankles.

Victor unlocked the door. He just wanted to get her inside and pull her into his arms. And what was up with that? He was hardly the coddling type.

He opened the suite door and ushered her inside.

"Slipping out at night, coming in long past dawn...This is hardly the way to keep a low profile..." At that low, mocking voice, Victor's body immediately went into battle mode. He pushed Zoe behind him and had his gun out in two seconds.

Drake raised his brows as he sat on the couch, not looking properly intimated. Did the guy just always get guns aimed at him? Was that why he was acting as if nothing new were happening at that moment?

"What the hell are you doing in here?" Victor demanded.

"It's my hotel." Drake kept lounging. "When you didn't answer the door, I got worried. Let myself in. You know, with the master key I have and all that."

Victor grunted.

"Going to lower the gun anytime soon?" Drake asked.

Zoe's fingers feathered over his back. "Victor, you know he's not a threat."

No, not a threat. But a serious asshole. Victor lowered his gun. Zoe slipped around him.

The mocking smile that *had* been on Drake's face vanished when he got a look at Zoe. "What in the hell happened?"

"That bad, huh?" Zoe muttered.

Victor put the gun back in its holster. "Drake, it's really been one pisser of a night."

Drake rose to his feet. "I'm getting that." His head cocked as he studied Zoe with concern. "What I *don't* get...is where did you two go? I thought you were planning to wait for my team to find Michelle—"

"Cancel that plan," Victor directed. "Just forget about her."

But Zoe stiffened. "No, no, we can't do that."

"Zoe." What now? "The woman is an undercover cop. She went off the radar for a reason. She wasn't who you thought. She was just—"

"Using me?" Zoe cut in with a sad smile. "I got that. Trust me, I got it. But Roy took me for a reason."

"Who the hell is Roy?" Drake asked, looking confused.

For the moment, Victor ignored him. "Roy took you for a lot of reasons. Two million of them."

Her cheeks reddened. "He said it wasn't just about the money. He said he had a chance to get Michelle back. You heard him—he was going to trade me for her!"

Victor wrapped his hands around her shoulders. "He's a cop who went bad. The guy got greedy, desperate for a big pay day. He isn't some hero trying to save the woman he loves. He's scum and you shouldn't believe his lies."

Her gaze searched his. "What if she is being held? What if her cover was blown?"

"No." He tightened his hold on her. "Just stop, right there. We are done, got it? You're done. You almost died."

Drake whistled. "Heavy night."

"You have no clue," Victor snapped back. Then his voice softened as he told Zoe, "We came to Vegas. We looked for her. Now we have to do some serious damage control—and focus on *you*."

Her lashes lowered.

"You should go…go take a hot bath and relax." That would be good, right? She'd been through hell, so she'd want to relax. Get the blood and ash off her. She'd—

Her lashes lifted, and the rage he saw in her stare froze him.

"Is that what you think of me?" Her voice was soft. Tight. "That I'll go all tra-la-la off and forget that Michelle exists? That she could be in danger right now?"

"She isn't the friend you thought—"

"No, she's not. She's a cop who was working an angle." Her eyes narrowed on him. "Just like you're an agent who's working one."

Shock rolled through him.

"What? You think I didn't know?" Bitterness was there, in her voice, on her face. "Come on,

Victor, you have to be working an angle with me. No way you've been helping me out of the kindness of your heart. If I go by what the other agents have said, you don't exactly have any kindness to offer."

He should stop touching her. He should pull back. He should say…something.

"You aren't denying it. But then, you don't have to deny it. I knew all along that you were holding back. Using me. When we were in that plane, and you started talking to me about Luther, I realized you were holding back even then. It's not just about getting *him* to cooperate, is it? It's about getting *me* to work with you. With the FBI."

"It…it isn't like that." Fuck, no, it wasn't like that. So why couldn't he explain it to her?

"Really?" But there wasn't any hope in her eyes as she continued. "Here's the thing…I knew you were working an angle. I still wanted you, though. I still fell for you. Got so caught up in you that I can barely think of my life without you."

She'd done what?

"I am not Luther Bates. I get punished for his sins all the time, but I'm not him." Her eyes gleamed at him. "So I can't walk away when someone's life is in danger. I can't just turn my back on Michelle, no matter what she's done. I will find a way to help her. And either I'll do it with you at my side…" Her lips twisted as she shrugged. "Or I'll do it on my own."

She stepped back, pulling away from him. "Now, I'm going to take a shower because I've been in a fire, I've been kidnapped, and I've been held hostage in some really smelly motel room. I want to get clean, and I want to figure out what move I'll be making next. Be sure of one thing though, I'm not just going to *relax*. So don't say that crap to me again."

Then she turned on her heel, kept her head up, and very gracefully walked out of the room. No storming. No stomping.

Pure fucking class.

The bathroom door shut behind her a few moments later. Victor was still standing there, staring after her, feeling as if he'd just been punched about a dozen times in the stomach — and by one fine fighter.

"That's…one hell of a woman." Drake's admiration was more than obvious.

"Screw off." He tossed a glare at the guy.

"I can see where she'd have you all tangled up. I mean…who doesn't like a smart, sexy, strong woman? Only a dumbass, obviously."

Victor narrowed his eyes on Drake.

Drake shrugged. "What? You know that's my type. How else would I have ended up so addicted to Jasmine?"

Victor's back teeth ground together.

"And I can see the signs," Drake added with a knowing nod. "You are a sinking ship, buddy. Might as well admit you're hooked on her."

"Drake…" A warning edge had entered his voice.

"I am curious…" Now Drake cocked his head as he studied Victor. "When did she stop being a case for you? Or have you been lying to yourself all this time? Thinking that you were working her when really…" His words trailed away.

"Really — what? By all means, don't stop there."

Drake's smile stretched. "When really, every second you were with her…that woman in there was stealing more and more of your heart."

She wasn't stealing it. I gave it to her. And now he was totally fucked.

"What matters more?" Drake asked as he stalked closer to Victor. "Her or the case?"

"It's not that easy," Victor gritted out. "There are things that you don't know."

"Make it that easy. Because you don't want to wind up like me, waking up one day and finding out that the woman you want most is gone."

Guilt twisted in Victor's stomach. He'd been responsible for that happening to Drake. *I was only trying to keep Jasmine safe.* "I'm not letting Zoe offer herself up in exchange for Michelle. I'm getting her out of Vegas. As soon as possible, I'm putting her on that jet of yours. I'll find a safe place for her."

That was all there was to it. He couldn't, wouldn't, risk her any longer.

***

Victor wasn't going to help her find Michelle. Not anymore.

Zoe knew it, with utter certainty. She'd seen the look on his face. Victor was probably already making plans to pack up and fly them out of Vegas. No doubt, he was already picking out some small little town to put her in. A new hiding spot.

She was tired of hiding.

She slipped out of the shower, the steam rising all around her. Her body ached, her head throbbed, but Zoe was alive, so she figured…what's the point in complaining?

She'd survived, again. Cheated death once more.

But she wasn't sure Michelle would be so lucky.

Zoe grabbed the big, fluffy, white robe that hung on a gleaming, silver hook in the bathroom. She slipped it on, pausing for just a moment because the thing was ridiculously soft.

Very, very nice.

Then Zoe took a deep breath. She squared her shoulders. Time to face Victor. Time to tell him that, hell, no, she wasn't running. It was her life, and if she wanted to help Michelle, she would. The last thing she needed was a cop's death on her conscience. Zoe opened the bathroom door and marched down the hallway, though her march didn't make much noise because of the thick carpeting.

When she left the hallway, she saw the man standing in front of the big window, gazing down at the city below. A tall man, with broad shoulders and…

Blond hair.

She staggered to a quick stop. "Where's Victor?"

Drake turned toward her. "He said he needed to talk with a cop."

"Without me?" Her voice rose. Anger did that, made her voice rise, made her feel all twitchy. "The jerk."

"Actually…" Drake walked toward her. "I'm supposed to keep watch over you while he's gone."

A hotel owner was her bodyguard? "Yes, well, thanks, but no thanks."

A hint of a smile curved his lips. "Don't be so dismissive. I promise, I've got some skill sets that would surprise you."

She wasn't touching that one.

"Victor Monroe is an interesting man," Drake mused.

"I think he can be a bit of an ass." Why not be honest? "Considering he just dumped me here right after my abduction."

"Definite ass." Drake appeared all too happy to agree with her. "But…you know why he left you here."

"Because he has an insane protection complex?"

"Because you matter to him."

She tightened the belt on her robe. "You sound as if you understand him."

"I'm probably as close to a…friend…as the guy has. But, believe me, we certainly didn't start things out that way. When I first met him, I pretty much hated the guy on sight. Victor and his secrets…they can do so much damage."

Zoe found herself inching closer to him. "Tell me…"

He lifted a brow.

"Tell me what he's really like. Tell me just how much he's jerking me around." Because she was a mess and when it came to Victor, she couldn't see clearly enough.

"He's not jerking you around, that I know for certain."

Her heart drummed faster.

"He's gone to the police station *for you*. Because Victor wants to get you on a jet and fly you out of this town."

She'd known that.

"But he also wants you happy. And finding out more about Michelle Lane, talking to some cop named Roy Duncan, well, Victor said he had to do it. For you."

Her breath heaved out. "He should have taken me with him!"

"Vic said there was already one bad cop in the mix. With that two million dollar bounty on your head, he couldn't risk others taking aim at you." Drake rocked back on his heels. "I've been ordered to stay with you until he gets back. And he *will* be back. Hopefully with some answers for you."

And she got to play the waiting game. Lovely. "That security team you sent out last night…did they discover anything?"

"Only that Michelle Lane disappeared from sight about a month after she started working at the Vine Casino."

"The Vine? I don't know that place."

"It's new. Started up by some corporation from back East. My men are digging up dirt on the place now."

Everyone seemed to be doing something. Everyone but her.

"I've got new clothes coming up for you," Drake said. "The delivery should be here any moment."

New clothes would be better than just hanging around in the robe all day. "Thanks." Zoe turned away from Drake.

"Don't trust him."

She stilled.

"I'm not supposed to say that, but I do *know* Victor. And even though the guy wants you, even though he seems to fucking need you, I've seen what he can do. The shit that happened to him when he was a kid messed him up. That need for justice that he has? I'd call it fanatical. And with your past…"

She looked back at him. "You mean my father."

Drake nodded. "Victor has been working on your father's case for a very long time. I know how much it means to him."

It means more to him than I do. She understood exactly what Drake was saying. And what he wasn't.

"Watch yourself with him," Drake added. "What you see…it's just not always what he really feels."

"Thanks for the warning." She made sure to keep any sadness or pain out of her voice. "But I already knew that if it came down to a choice…me or the case…" Zoe laughed. "Well, I knew there wouldn't be a choice, not for Victor."

***

"Tell me what's happening." Victor slapped his hands down on Cain Blair's desk and glowered at the guy. "I just got some bullshit story from your captain about no one having access to Roy Duncan. He said Internal Affairs was coming in to talk with the guy, and that no one else would have access until they were done."

Cain looked up from his computer. A line of stubble coated the guy's jaw. *Hell, I bet I have the same shit on mine.* He was running on pure adrenaline and rage, and Victor got that he was long past the point of any kind of control.

"I don't think the FBI has jurisdiction here," Cain murmured carefully. "Though I am glad you hauled your butt in here. I need statements from you. And Zoe." He rose, looking over Victor's shoulder. "Where is she?"

"Like I'd tell you — or any cop in this place."

Cain's jaw hardened. "I didn't know I was working with a traitor. Get that shit straight."

"I want to talk to him."

"The captain is calling the shots, not me. I wish I could help you, but I can't."

Not what Victor wanted to hear. "Roy told Zoe that he was going to trade her for Michelle."

Cain's eyelids flickered.

"You said she went dark. *Roy* was willing to kidnap and kill because he thought Michelle's life was on the line. If you've got a cop out there — one who is in mortal danger — why the hell isn't your captain acting?"

"Because he's afraid everything is about to blow up in his face!" Cain glanced angrily toward the captain's closed office door. "The guy knows that he should have pulled Michelle at the first sign of trouble. He didn't. And now he's trying to cover his ass."

"I can get you FBI assistance." Victor kept his voice calm with a supreme effort. "I can help you, but first you have to help me."

Cain yanked a hand through his hair. "Why are you still in town? I figured you'd vanish as soon as you had your lady back."

He did want to vanish. But… "Zoe came here to find her friend. She's even more convinced now that Michelle is in danger."

Surprise widened Cain's eyes. "But she knows Michelle is a cop."

"Doesn't matter. Zoe wants to find her."

Cain's hand lowered to rest near his holster. "And let me guess…you want to make Zoe happy, right? If she gets what she wants, then she's more likely to trust you. To cooperate with you. To turn on her father and do whatever the hell you—"

"I don't want her crying because her friend is dead." Cold, brutal. "I don't want her hurting because she blames herself for something happening to Michelle."

Cain seemed to absorb that.

"So you going to work with me?" Victor waved his hand around the precinct. "Or should I just go over your captain's head, too? Maybe the FBI *does* need to take jurisdiction. I'm sure I can. After all, it was my case that was jeopardized. My *witness* that was taken and nearly killed."

"Dammit…" Cain's frustration was obvious.

Victor smiled at him. "Get me face-to-face with Roy. Do it now or I will use every bit of pull I have to take total control here." Yeah, he was a bastard, and, right then, he didn't care.

Zoe. I'm doing this for Zoe.

This…and so much more.

* * *

"Five minutes," Cain muttered as he directed Victor toward an isolated cell in the back of the holding area. "We have five minutes back here, and then our asses are toast."

Victor looked through those bars and saw Roy rising to his feet. He gave the bastard a grim smile. "I guess we meet again."

"No!" Roy held up his hands. "I'm not talking to you. I'm not talking to *anyone* but my lawyer." His face was bruised, one eye nearly shut. His nose swollen. His upper lip busted.

"Do you really care about Michelle?" Victor asked him. "Or was that some bullshit line you fed Zoe?"

Roy jumped toward the bars. "I *love* her!"

So much for talking only to his lawyer. With guys like Roy, it was all about knowing which buttons to push. "You love her *and* the two million you were going to get for Zoe?"

"Michelle was going to die!" Spittle flew from Roy's mouth. "What was I supposed to do? Zoe was made when she headed into Dice. The wrong person saw her. Why do you think that other hitter was already in the alley? She was *made*. In this town, danger is always two fucking steps behind you, so you have to learn how to walk real fast."

Victor had wondered about that man in the alley. Had the hitman been in the shadows of Dice? Just outside, watching? But Victor would question that would-be shooter, soon enough. For now, his focus was on Roy.

Roy's cheeks flushed. "I got a call from some guy, okay? Right after you two made the mistake of going into Dice. Fellow said he was at the Vine. Guy promised me that if I brought Zoe to him, then Michelle could live *and* I'd get the pay."

Cain was silent. Did he buy the guy's story? Victor didn't. "The Vine…" Victor repeated the name even as he made the connection. He'd seen the sign for the place when he and Zoe first arrived in town.

"*That's* where Michelle went to work," Roy said quickly. "That casino — it's a front, I know it. And when I got the call, telling me to bring Zoe if I ever wanted to see Michelle again, I-I just stopped thinking clearly. Panic took over."

"When did you get the call?"

"Like I already told you — right after you walked into Dice." He licked his lips. "Someone saw Zoe. Someone made the connection. I was told to get her, and I did."

"When was the exchange supposed to take place?"

Roy's stare jerked between him and Cain. "What will happen to me?" Roy asked. "I was a good cop…"

"*When was the exchange supposed to take place?*"

"I don't know! I was told I'd get another call. That's what I was waiting for at that motel! But then you assholes took me into custody!" His voice rose as he yanked on the bars. "So I didn't get the second call! I didn't make the trade! And Michelle is going to *die!*"

Was the guy telling the truth? Or just making a desperate attempt to dig himself out of the serious shit-hole he'd already dug? Victor gave a grim nod. "Okay, let's go back and take this story from—"

"You're not taking anything." The voice was smooth, smug, and coming from right behind him. "My client is done talking with you."

Hell. He should have known that a lawyer would show up to spoil his fun. Victor threw a glance over his shoulder. "If your client wants to keep talking, that's his choice."

The brown-haired male in the suit that reeked of money smiled a bit, a faint curving of his lips. That smile didn't reach his cold eyes. "My client isn't talking because I don't want him spending the rest of his life in a prison surrounded by inmates who want nothing more than to get payback on the cop in their midst."

"*Oh, Jesus,*" Roy mumbled. "Jesus."

"You're done here," the lawyer said to Victor. "I need to confer with my client."

Victor turned to fully face the attorney. His gaze swept over the man, head to toe, taking his stock, not liking the guy at all with his stiff posture and cold eyes. "Didn't catch your name," Victor murmured.

"And I didn't catch yours." But the lawyer stepped forward, offering his hand.

Victor took that hand. "FBI Special Agent Victor Monroe."

Once again, that faint smile appeared. Only this time, the lawyer's eyes hardened. "I'm Xavier Winters. But my friends call me Tom."

Sonofabitch.

***

He was so screwed.

Roy Duncan hunched over against the cell bars. He'd thought that he could get away clean. Get the money. Get his girl. And ride away into the sunset.

Now his ass was locked in a jail cell.

Cops couldn't go to prison. Everyone knew that. Everyone knew the shit that waited for them in those hellholes. He couldn't go down like that. There had to be a way out.

Footsteps padded on the concrete floor. His eyes locked on the dark-haired guy heading his way — the guy who'd identified himself as Roy's attorney. Only the problem was that Roy had never seen that man in his life. The fellow sure as shit *wasn't* his lawyer.

"Now that the FBI agent is gone, how about we talk privately?" The attorney smiled at him. Some dude in a fancy suit, with perfect features and an old money vibe rolling off him. As Roy stared at the fellow, the lawyer's head inclined toward the uniformed cop who watched from a nearby corner. "Total privacy would be best."

Roy got the message, loud and clear. The attorney wanted the uniform gone. Fine. Roy nodded. "Leave us alone," he told the cop.

The uniform hesitated.

"I'm locked up! What the hell do you think I'll do? Give us privacy!" Because Roy wanted to know who this fellow was…

And how he could use him.

The uniform glared at Roy, but backed away.

The *lawyer* smirked at Roy.

"Xavier Winters," Roy murmured, trying to place the name but coming up blank. "Funny, I don't remember hiring you."

Xavier laughed. "That's probably a good thing because, you see, my normal rates are very, very high."

What was going on?

"But don't worry. I have a special deal for you, Officer Duncan." Xavier sidled closer to the bars. "I think you and I can help each other."

"How the hell are you supposed to help me?" *Try bribing a judge. Maybe that would work.*

The lawyer straightened his already straight tie. "I can make sure you never see the inside of a prison."

Now *those* words sure caught Roy's attention. "Keep talking."

"No, actually, *you're* the one who needs to talk." Xavier locked his gaze on Roy's. "Tell me everything you know about Zoe Peters. Every. Single. Thing."

***

"Was that everything you hoped and more?" Cain drawled as he and Victor marched away from holding. "Because to me, it sure seemed that we got jackshit out of the guy."

Xavier Winters. It was no coincidence that the lawyer had shown up. "I got plenty I can use." Just by seeing Winters. His eyes sharpened on Cain. "I want to see the shooter you arrested in that alleyway. Maybe he can tell us who hired him for the hit."

Cain's lips thinned. "Right this way."

The guy wasn't going to argue with him? No bitching about case territory this time? Victor hurried to follow Cain down the hallway, but they weren't heading back to holding. Cain took him downstairs. Down, down below to…

"What in the hell?"

A body was tagged and bagged down there, and an ME stood to the side, tapping on a laptop.

"There's the shooter," Cain said, voice tight. "Within five minutes of him getting to booking, another prisoner had knifed him. The guy will be telling you *nothing*."

Victor shook his head.

"*That's* why Roy is in holding alone. Because we suspect there's already orders pending to have him killed, too." Cain rolled back his shoulders. "But, hey, I'm newer to this game than you are, so you tell me...you think Luther Bates could really have already heard about the attack on his daughter? Do you really think that man's reach is so strong that he could've had the shooter killed the instant he came into this place? Or..." Cain blew out a rough breath. "Do you think someone *else* ordered the shooter taken out? Maybe the power player we're after in Vegas?"

"Even Luther couldn't get a hit moving on the shooter this fast." At least, he didn't think so. Luther couldn't, but someone in Vegas could, someone pulling the strings in this city...*puppet master*. "Your power player is one busy asshole." And Victor would be stopping him. "Better double the guards on Roy," Victor advised darkly. "Or he may not make it through the night."

CHAPTER TWELVE

When the hotel room door opened hours later, Zoe felt as if she were about to explode. Victor strode inside, looking all tall, dark, and dangerous, and she wanted to rage at him.

Drake Archer had proven himself to be a very annoying opponent. She'd tried — at least three times — to give the guy the slip.

Not happening. Either Drake — or his security goons — had found a way to stop her each time. And he'd kept her trapped in the suite.

"I kept my promise," Drake said as he rose languidly from the couch. "She didn't get away."

Victor gave a jerky nod. "You don't even realize what an accomplishment that is."

Her teeth were clenched so tightly her jaw ached.

"Yes, well," Drake mused, "I learned from Jasmine's work. Wasn't about to make the same mistake again."

Victor met Zoe's stare. He winced. "So you're seriously pissed?"

"Pissed doesn't do me justice." Not even close.

"Will it help if I say that I found out information we can use?"

She rose. Didn't leap at him. Didn't scream. Zoe just stood there and softly said, "You cut me out."

"*I wanted to protect you.*"

"You cut me out," she repeated. "Don't ever do it again. If you do…"

Victor's eyes glittered.

"I'll walk." He should know that she meant those words. "I'll vanish. Sure, maybe Drake kept me here today, but we both know…I can eventually get away. I will *always* get away. So whatever intel you *hope* you're going to get from me about Luther, it won't happen if you shut me out again. I won't be left in the dark."

He rushed toward her. Reached for her but stopped. "You think I can't see that I'm screwing things to hell and back with you?" His voice was low, ragged. "I see it. I know it, but I don't know how to stop. I want you safe. I want to give you everything you need. I just don't fucking know how."

There was pain in his words. Pain and confusion and he seemed so lost.

As lost as she felt.

"What if another cop there had been tempted by the two million?" Victor asked. "I couldn't do it, Zoe. I couldn't risk you, so I went to the station on my own. I wanted to learn something that would help Michelle. Help you. I swear, baby, I never meant to hurt you."

Drake cleared his throat. "Okay, so you two have lots to work out—obviously—but how about we focus on the part about Michelle for a bit? What happened when you got to the station, Vic? Did you throw your big, bad, annoying FBI weight around—as you and I both know you like to do—and find out anything else about the woman?"

The faint lines near Victor's eyes deepened. "She went to work as a showgirl at the Vine."

"Yes, yes, we know that," Drake muttered. "I meant did you find out something *new*?"

"She went to work at the Vine, only she never danced," Victor continued, his voice sounding tired. "I talked to Cain about her. Seems she spent all her time with upper management. Behind closed doors. She was working her way to the top. Trying to find out who was the power behind the corporate front...because that power is the new crime boss in town."

"He's the one she sold me out to," Zoe said. He had to be the one.

Victor nodded. "And all signs at the Vegas PD point to him being the one who has the hits on you. That fool hitman that Cain stopped in the alley? He's already dead because someone wanted to make sure he didn't talk."

Zoe's hand rose to her throat. *When would the bodies ever stop piling up?*

"I did get that bastard Roy to reveal some information, and everything he said just pointed back to the Vine."

"Then we need to get in there." They should be storming the place right then. "We have to search there and see what we can find out about Michelle."

Victor shook his head. "The cops can't get in. Not yet. They're waiting for orders from above."

"I'm not a cop." So she didn't have to wait for any orders from above. "We can do this, Victor. You and me. We can get in there and help her. If you want to make this whole abandonment mess up to me…*then we will work together on this.*"

Victor's gaze was so bright. So intense. "Drake," he said, without glancing away from Zoe. "Leave us, would you?"

"Already heading for the door."

Zoe wrapped her arms around her stomach.

The suite's door opened.

"Thank you," Victor called out. The words seemed a bit rusty.

"Anytime." Just like that, Drake was gone.

And she was locked in a face-off with Victor.

"I'm afraid for you," he confessed.

Those words were the last she'd expected to hear from him. Zoe shook her head in automatic denial. She had a hard time imagining Victor being afraid about anything.

"The people in the Vine...they want to kill you," Victor said.

"Yeah, I got that."

"Zoe, you're coming too close to death. Don't do this. Don't ask this shit of me." Victor strode closer to her. His body wasn't touching hers, but she could feel the heat that seemed to cling to him. "Cain and his crew can handle the search for Michelle. They've got this case covered."

Zoe shook her head. "They don't have me. Roy said he could trade me for Michelle. I'm the ticket we need to get her out alive."

His eyes closed. "What am I supposed to fucking do?"

"You're supposed to be at my side, helping me stay alive." She reached out and curled her fingers around his hand. "We can do this. Together. We can come up with a plan that will work, I know we can."

He looked at their joined hands. "I won't be able to handle it if something happens to you. When I couldn't find you after the fire, I swear, it was like something flipped off inside of me. I wasn't...I wasn't quite sane."

"How do you think I felt when I woke up in that little motel room, and I didn't know if you were alive or dead?" She squeezed his hand. "The whole world went dark on me right then."

His head snapped back. His eyes locked on hers. "Be careful, Zoe."

She stood on her tip-toes and pressed a kiss to his lips. "Why? I've got a special agent to keep me safe."

"Be careful with me. I'm wanting you too much."

"Is it possible to want someone *too* much?" She wanted him right then. Wanted him in her. Wanted the reassurance that they were both safe. Alive.

Together.

"You don't want me to lose control."

Actually, that was exactly what she wanted. Zoe swallowed and said, "I didn't think the great Victor Monroe ever lost at anything."

"I do." His voice was grim. "Trust me, I fucking do."

Staring hard into his gaze, she said, "I do trust you."

Surprise flashed on his face.

"I thought, maybe, it was time you knew that," she whispered the confession to him.

His head lowered toward hers. His mouth pressed against her lips. Softly. Carefully. "What are you doing to me?"

I have no idea.

"You are blowing my plans to hell." His words were angry, but his mouth was so careful on hers. "And I don't even care." He licked her lower lip. "I can't stop…with you, I can't."

Was that good? Or bad? "Victor…"

His head lifted. "If you didn't have a concussion, I would be fucking you as hard as I could right now."

The concussion? What concussion? She felt fine, and it had been *hours* since he'd forced her to stop in at that hospital.

But he pulled away from her and stalked toward the window. He seemed to be staring so hard at the gleaming Vegas lights. "Sometimes, I hate my job."

She rubbed her chilled arms. The chill had come from the coldness of his voice. "I thought you liked upholding the peace. Stopping the bad guys." She tried to make her voice sound light, but Zoe knew she failed.

"Some bad guys…they get beneath your skin. They twist the world around them. If you're not careful, they'll twist you."

The drumming of her heartbeat filled her ears. "You're talking about Luther."

He was still not looking at her. "He's one of the coldest SOBs I've ever met."

Her father *was* the coldest SOB she'd ever met. No doubt about it.

"We can't ever let him get out of prison, Zoe. Help me make sure that doesn't happen."

She could barely breathe. The idea of her father, loose…

"How many people will he kill…" Victor continued, "once he's on the street?"

Her gaze fell to the floor. Guilt cut through her, the way it always did when she thought of all the terrible things her father had done.

Like father, like daughter…

"There's something else."

But she didn't want to hear anything else right then.

"More is at play in Vegas than we realize. More that involves *you*." His footsteps padded toward her. His fingers curled under her chin, and he tilted her head back. His touch was so gentle as he gazed down at her. "Your ex, Tom Winters…"

"You told me he was in Vegas." She tried to keep her voice even. "It's not like we're going to see him—"

"Yeah, I already *have* seen him."

"What? When?"

"While I was questioning Roy, Tom arrived. Seems he's Roy's attorney, too."

"No." An automatic denial. Tom couldn't be working for Luther *and* for Roy. There was no way coincidences like that happened.

It's not a coincidence.

Victor's gaze was solemn. "The players in this game are lining up."

Not a game. Don't call it that.

"And I don't like what's happening. I don't like what I think could be coming."

Luther Bates. Tom. Planning some kind of legal twist to get my father out of prison.

"We need to work together, Zoe. You said you trusted me — keep trusting me. I will help you get Michelle. I will stand by your side through whatever hell might come our way."

He already had. He'd been risking his life for her, again and again.

"And I *will* protect you from the thing that you fear the most."

She stared into his eyes. Zoe gazed deep and saw that he'd uncovered her darkest secret.

The thing she feared most in the whole world...

It was her father.

"Once Michelle is safe..." She exhaled a ragged breath. "I'll do everything I can to help you keep my father in jail." *My father.*

She saw the satisfaction flash across his face. But she wondered — did he have any idea just how much the deal would cost her?

***

Cops could be such pains in the ass. Xavier—Tom—Winters made sure to keep his casual smile in place as he left the station. Every eye in the place had been on him. What had they expected? That he'd slip up right there? It wasn't amateur hour.

His driver was waiting at the curb, standing in front of that long, sleek ride as if he were waiting for a celebrity. *That's what I am now.* Tom nodded to him as he climbed into the back. The door shut behind him and Tom started to reach for his phone, but then he stopped.

No need to check-in. He had this covered. Everything was moving along perfectly.

FBI Special Agent Victor Monroe was back in town, and that meant, of course…that Zoe Peters was close. The guy had her stashed someplace. That wouldn't do. Zoe needed to come into the open.

The better for me to see. The better for me to touch.

Zoe didn't understand just how many lives were on the line. The woman also didn't get that she was being used. Coldly. Brilliantly.

That was Zoe's problem, though. She didn't have her father's killer instinct. From what Tom could tell, she had *no* killer instinct. Zoe wanted to save the world, to atone for all of Luther's sins.

Not happening.

His fingers tapped against his phone. There were plenty of ways he could handle the situation, but why not just go for the direct route?

FBI Special Agent Victor Monroe.

He *was* the direct route. Good thing Tom had already done plenty of research on Victor Monroe. That had been Luther's primary directive to him.

Tear apart Monroe's past. Find his every weak spot.

Then exploit the hell out of that weakness.

His eyes closed as he leaned back against the leather seat. After his little chat with Roy, he had a pretty good idea of exactly what Victor's weakness might be. And Tom knew that he didn't have to go out and hunt Victor and Zoe…

They'll be coming to me.

***

"Zoe…" She turned at the low whisper of her name. She'd been waiting all day for Victor to work out the arrangements on their plan. He'd been calling in favors at the FBI, making sure that *he* took over jurisdiction in Vegas.

It was almost time to act. *Michelle, please, hold on.*

"I have something for you." He stood in the doorway. *Her* bedroom. The suite had two bedrooms. This was the first time he'd walked into her room. He lifted up the box he held in his arms. Some fancy box with a high end store name written in script on the side.

She stared at that box as if it were a snake. "You got me a present?" She couldn't remember the last time someone had done that, and she sure didn't know how to act. "Victor?" She looked at his face.

And saw his shock. His pain.

He put the box down. Went to her. Took her hands in his. "You deserve so much."

Embarrassment flooded her cheeks. "It's not a present. It's for the-the case, right? I mean, I know, I—"

He kissed her. Deep. Hard. Hot.

She moaned into his mouth. Desire beat in her blood. When he started to pull back, she twisted her hands, holding onto him then. "Don't be a tease."

His eyes glittered down at her. "I'm not teasing."

"It's been twenty-four hours since I got the bump on the head." Twenty-four long hours. "I am *fine*. And before anything else happens…" Another attack, their recuse attempt with Michelle…whatever hell might be waiting. "I want to be with you."

A muscle jerked in his jaw.

"Don't you want to be with me?"

"More than I want my next breath."

Her breath caught. "That's an awful lot," she murmured. Her hands rose to curl around his shoulders. She pulled him closer. "I want a present."

His eyelids flickered.

"I want you. I'm asking for you. Right now, give yourself to me, Victor. Totally." She eased out a slow breath. "Because that's the same way I'll give myself to you." No holding back, not for either of them.

She could see the desire in his eyes. Good.

She pulled off his shirt. Tossed it across the room. Then her hands went to the snap of his jeans. The hiss of his zipper seemed loud, and then she was pushing down the denim. He wasn't wearing underwear and his cock—already heavy with arousal—sprang into her hands. She slipped to her knees before him.

"Zoe…"

And she took him into her mouth. Her tongue swiped over the head of his arousal. She licked him. She pumped. She loved the way he felt in her mouth. But, more, she loved the way he tasted. That sweet drop of—

With careful hands, he pulled her to her feet. Then he pushed her onto the bed. He stripped her, slowly, gently, even as the breath heaved from his lungs and the desire in his eyes blazed ever brighter.

She was naked before him. Her body completely open and he put his hands between her thighs, spreading her even more for him. Her breasts were aching, the nipples tight, and she was already wet for him. Ready.

Victor put his mouth on her. Her breath rushed out on a heavy moan when he started licking her. The man's tongue…his lips…

She fisted the covers and fought the orgasm that was building within her. This time, she wanted to come— "With you in me!" The demand broke from her. "Please, Victor, I want you *in me!*"

His head lifted. His expression had gone primitive. He left the bed. Left her.

Her body ached. "Victor?"

But he came back moments later. He ripped open the condom pack in his hand. Put the condom on in damn near record time.

She started to smile, but the dark lust on his face…it stilled her smile.

He climbed onto the bed. Pinned her hands near her head. "You can't move too much," he ordered. "You have to take it easy."

She didn't want to be easy. Her chin lifted. "And you have to take *me*."

"Always," he promised her.

Then he thrust into her. Thick. Full. Hot. He withdrew, plunged deep, and set them on a fast and hard rhythm. She didn't try to stop her climax this time. She let herself go. Trusted Victor completely. The pleasure hit her and she couldn't even cry out his name. She was lost, so swept away, so free—

And he was with her. He shuddered against her and bellowed Zoe's name. She stared up at him and saw the pleasure flash on his face. So much pleasure.

The same soul-searing climax that she felt.

***

"Zoe." Victor stroked her cheek. She was in bed with him. Her body so soft and relaxed. She'd slept in his arms. He'd stayed awake, wanting to hold her close always.

Always.

"Zoe." This time, he said her name a little louder.

She stretched against him and her eyes opened.

"I have some presents for you."

"What?"

She'd nearly broken his heart before. With the look on her face…the wistfulness in her voice.

I want to give her the world. And all I've done is set her up for pain. He cleared his throat. "I got Russell to do a little shopping for us. He arrived in town earlier—along with the rest of our FBI back-up. The guy knows where to find some really good toys."

She sat up in bed, pulling the sheet to her neck. "Are you talking about sex toys?"

If only. He shook his head, and he offered her the stack of boxes that he'd gotten Russell to pick up for them.

Hesitantly, she reached for the first box.

"We'll be going to the Vine soon," Victor said. Because the thing Zoe wanted most? Michelle's life. Her safety. And if Zoe wanted them to free the woman, then they would. *But I will do everything to protect Zoe.* "So I wanted you to be ready."

She opened the box. "Um, Victor…did you just give me a knife?"

He lifted it out of the box. "It's small enough to hide easily on your body. Most people wouldn't find it during a search."

Zoe blinked.

"I want you safe," Victor said clearly. "I *need* you safe." The knife wasn't much, but it was better than nothing. Zoe always should have a way to protect herself.

"Thank you."

He handed her the second box.

"You know," Zoe mused as she held the box. "Most men give women diamond earrings. At least, that's what I heard lovers do."

She opened the box.

Diamond earrings glittered up at her.

"Victor?"

He wished they were just diamond earrings. A gift from a lover without any strings. He rolled back his shoulders. "There's a listening device on this one. A very, very small transmitter." He tapped the earring that was slightly bigger. "Wear it in your right ear. I'll have a listening device on me, too. We'll use mine first, and yours will be back-up. Just in case..."

"In case what?"

"In case we become separated when we go into the Vine."

She paled. "Right." Fumbling, she put the earrings in place. Then her gaze darted to the last box. "I think I'm scared to see what's inside there."

He gave her the box. A very big box.

Zoe bit her lower lip and slowly, so slowly, opened the box. In it were—

"Feathers?" Zoe laughed. She pulled out the feathers. "My old showgirl costume! Victor, how did you—"

"I just wanted something to make you smile. When you were on the plane, you seemed so happy when you talked about dancing." He spoke gruffly. "It's...not a big deal. I just thought you'd like to have it, that's all."

Oh, hell, it looked as if she might start to cry.

"I can get rid of it," Victor said quickly. "I can—"

She threw her arms around him. Held tight. "Thank you, Victor."

Slowly, his own arms rose to hold her. It was strange, but she seemed to feel…right…against him.

"The costume does make me happy, but *you* make me happier."

He didn't know what to say. Zoe eased back and stared up at him. "Thank you," she said once more.

"You don't need to thank me. Hell, I'm the idiot who is letting you walk into danger. I should be sending you away."

"No. You're the good guy, Victor. Helping someone in need, that's kind of your thing." She rose from the bed, still holding the costume tightly. She squeezed it a moment, as if gaining courage, then she said, "So want to tell me the plan?"

The big plan.

"It's simple. Got to give credit to Roy Duncan. He inspired it."

Zoe just stared back at him.

"We go in the Vine together. Make a big entrance." He nodded toward the box on the dresser. The box he'd originally brought in to her hours before and Zoe had asked if it was a present. Now, he strode to that box. Opened it and pulled out the dress inside. "You'll wear this. Every eye in the place will be on you."

"And we want that?"

Grimly, he nodded. "We want you to catch the right attention."

"You mean the wrong attention."

Yeah, he did. "Before it's too late, are you *sure* this is what you want to do?"

She put down her feathered costume. Walked slowly toward him and reached for the dress. "Yes. Because I am *not* like my father. I won't let someone just die. *I won't.*"

No, that wasn't who Zoe was. He gazed down at her, wishing that things were different. Wishing that he didn't have secrets and lies between them.

"Victor? What is it? Why do you look so sad?"

Fuck. He glanced away. "It's time for us to go, Zoe." And time for him to do his job.

Falling for her wasn't the plan. But it's too late. Too late for us both.

CHAPTER THIRTEEN

The Vine. Decadent. Massive.

Criminal.

Victor strode inside the casino. Night had fallen, the perfect time to launch their rescue bid. All of the FBI agents he needed were in place for this operation. And, despite Cain Blair's fury, the FBI *had* swooped in, taking over jurisdiction in this case.

The Vine was no low end casino. It was a place that tailored to the wealthy. From the gleaming marble floor beneath his feet to the massive chandelier over his head — every inch of the place screamed money.

A lot of it.

Money that he and his team knew hadn't exactly come from legal sources.

"Are you sure you're ready for this?" Victor murmured. His gaze cut to her and shit, for a moment, he could only stare.

He'd thought Zoe was beautiful. He'd *known* she was beautiful. But tonight…tonight her long, dark hair tumbled around her shoulders. Make-up made her eyes smolder and her red lips gleam.

And her body…

Holy fuck. He'd had no idea the red dress would look so amazing on her. It hugged her body so perfectly. It was a dress that made him hard and desperate.

One that made him…

Want her. More than ever.

He wanted to forget the mission. Forget the whole freaking end-goal. He wanted to take her out of there. To just vanish with her.

To vanish, while she still looked at him as if he were some kind of hero. When Victor knew he was far, far from that.

"I'm ready." Her lips curved upward, but the smile didn't reach her eyes. The diamond earrings glittered on her ear lobes. Her listening device wasn't activated, not yet. Per his order. He'd shown her how to turn it on, though. A quick depression to activate. Another to turn the transmitter off.

When the time was right, he'd get her to use those earrings.

Victor knew the video cameras in that place were running. He saw the small security devices strategically located throughout the casino. Victor was sure that he and Zoe would be catching attention very soon.

In this place, the right people would know exactly who she was.

And what she was worth.

Her arm was wrapped around his. She walked beside him, poised, confident, breath-takingly sexy.

"You have the knife, right?" Victor asked her as they began to climb the long, spiral staircase that led to the second level of the casino. A giant, glittering Christmas tree — had to be at least twenty feet tall — stood at the base of that staircase.

"Yes," she said, her voice husky and soft. "For at least the tenth time, I have the knife. It's hidden in my bra."

He almost smiled. His crew was listening to every word that he said, thanks to the device that he wore. Other agents and cops were already *inside* the casino. In fact, he'd just caught a glimpse of Cain, looking calm and relaxed as he lifted a glass of champagne and flirted with a scantily-clad waitress.

They reached the top of the stairs. He saw a security guard watching them, a man wearing a light gray suit coat who stared at Zoe with narrowed eyes.

"Whatever happens," Victor said, "we stay together."

He made his way to the craps table. Zoe was at his side. He made a show of kissing her hand right before he put down a bet. When he won, instantly doubling his money, Victor smiled broadly at the crowd around him. "She's my good luck charm."

He set up another bet. Kissed her hand once more, and reached for the dice...

Another win.

The group at the table cheered. Zoe was silent and the guard who'd been watching him... the guy was on the move. The guard touched his ear piece and spoke softly as he closed in on Victor.

Guess it's show time.

Because he did love a good game, Victor threw the dice once more. Only this time, he lost. While the group murmured sympathetically, Victor just smiled. "The house has the advantage." *But not for long.*

The guard tapped his shoulder. "Sir, may I have a moment?"

Zoe stiffened next to him.

Once more, Victor caught her hand. He kissed her knuckles and gave her fingers a little squeeze. *It's okay, baby. I have this. You can trust me.*

He wasn't going to let her down. When he'd had Zoe in bed with him, safe in his arms, his mind had finally cleared and he'd realized what he needed to do.

Somehow, someway, he was going to keep her at his side. When the smoke cleared from this case, he wouldn't lose her. He couldn't. Zoe mattered. Simple fact.

Zoe. Mattered.

"Sir?" The guard pressed.

Victor glanced at him. "You guys have a rule here against losing?"

The guard's expression was tense. "You've been invited to the VIP lounge." His gaze cut to Zoe. "You and the lovely lady."

"VIP, huh?" He curled his arm around Zoe's waist and brought her in closer to him. Victor was wired with the smallest of devices, and he knew that both the FBI guys and Cain's crew would be hearing every word uttered right then. "How can we pass up on an invitation like that one?"

The guard's expression never changed. "You can't."

No, he hadn't thought that they could.

The guard turned on his heel and marched toward the elevator bank on the right.

"Not very friendly, is he?" Zoe murmured.

"I don't think friendliness is high on his priority list." He didn't hurry after the guy. Victor just took his time strolling casually through the crowd. Keeping Zoe close.

The guard didn't go to the main line of elevators. He walked past them, then stopped at an elevator that was accessible only with a keycard. He swiped his card, and the doors opened. The guard motioned for Victor and Zoe to step inside.

The doors began to close.

Zoe's hand flew out, triggering the sensors. "What happens in the VIP lounge?"

The guard—a guy who looked around twenty-five—gave a rough sigh. "Heaven." What could have been sympathy flashed in his eyes. "Or hell."

Zoe's hand fell back to her side. The doors closed and the elevator began to ascend.

Victor turned her body fully into his arms, then he leaned in close, putting his mouth near her ear. He knew security cameras were in that elevator. Cameras and the hotel's audio recording devices. So he made sure to keep his voice as the barest of whispers as he said, "Keep trusting me."

Her fingers rose and squeezed his shoulders. "I will."

Had any words ever been as fucking sweet? Especially since…hell, he was supposed to walk in there and act as if he were ready to sell her out. To trade her.

Two million dollars for Zoe Peters. That was the plan.

That wasn't enough money. Not even close.

They went straight up to the penthouse level. The elevator doors opened with the softest of dings.

Victor wasn't surprised to see the two guards standing there, both of them with ear pieces and hard, glinting stares. He gave them a grim smile. "Oh, look, honey," he drawled. "It's the VIP welcome crew."

One guard motioned him forward. "I need to search you."

Victor had expected nothing less. He lifted his hands so the pat down could begin. One guard was big, brawny — that would be the one searching him. The other guy was slender, more hesitant. That would be the guy lightly skimming his hands over Zoe.

Victor's eyes narrowed on him. "Just where the fuck…" he said, his voice gravel rough as fury pumped through him. "Do you think she'd hide a weapon?" Talking while the guy searched would serve to better distract the fellow.

The guy stilled. His gaze jerked to Victor. "Y-you'd be surprised at the things I see."

Victor growled back at him.

"Sh-she's clean," the guy said quickly. *Nice half-assed search.* The guy hadn't even found Zoe's knife.

Big and Brawny finished his search on Victor. "He's good, too. Send them in to the boss."

About damn time. Once more, Victor curled his arm around Zoe's waist. But before he strode forward, he glanced at the two guards. "What are your names?"

"Why?" Big and Brawny demanded.

Victor shrugged. "Because I always like to know the names of the assholes I meet?" *So the agents listening can learn more about you two.*

The guy grunted. "I'm Samuel, and this guy's Kevin, and you screw with us...we *will* break your face."

"Good to know." *I'd like to see you try.*

Samuel led them down a narrow hallway. No noise from the casino reached this level—they were far too high for that, and Victor suspected the walls there had been sound proofed. The guard turned to the right, opened a door, and directed them inside. Victor went first, ready to look for any threat, but the room—one that sported floor to ceiling windows everywhere he looked—was empty.

"Sit tight," the guard told him. "You'll have company soon." He pointed to the bar. "Help yourself."

Right. Because Victor wanted to get all liquored up for this little meeting.

Show me the boss. Bring the asshole in here to me so the Feds can swarm this place. That was the goal. Do their little show and dance. Get the guy to take the bait, and then...

It's over.

The door closed softly behind the guard. Zoe's breath rushed out. She looked up at him. "How do we know that they didn't bring us up here just to kill us both? Obviously, I was recognized the minute when I walked into the place."

Yeah, they'd counted on that. Counted on her face being picked up in the security feeds and identified immediately. What better way to cut through the red tape and get an appointment with the man in charge?

The man who could take them to Michelle. *If she's still alive.*

Though he hadn't said those words to Zoe, not yet. Because he didn't want her hope to die.

"No one will kill us." At least, not without one hell of a fight. Big and Brawny might not have found a weapon on him, but that didn't mean Victor wasn't armed. It just meant the guy hadn't looked well enough.

Patdowns were always the same. The guys usually went straight for the ribs, the hips, the upper legs. When searching a man, the patdown always made sure to include a sweep of the jacket. Obvious choice.

And if you happened to be carrying a gun or a large knife, those patdowns *would* result in finding hidden weapons. But those patdowns also sure as hell wouldn't turn up...

The weapons in his wallet. An old trick he'd learned — back on the streets when he'd been a punk ass kid — credit cards could be great, quick weapons. With some tape, a credit card, and a single edge razor, he'd made himself a fine and simple weapon — one that folks wouldn't even notice until it was too late. Victor also had a small knife tucked inside his belt. And plenty of other little surprises…

Like a stun gun that looked just like a smart phone. A pen in his coat pocket hid another knife. He'd always been a fan of extra weapons — they'd sure come in handy for him plenty of times. Spy tech was one of his obsessions.

"Cameras are watching us, right?"

He gave the briefest of nods. His gaze scanned the room. A desk waited a few feet away. Were they in the boss's office? Sure looked that way. *So come on in for our private meeting.*

As if on cue, the door opened once more. Victor's muscles locked down as another surge of adrenaline shot through him.

"Hello, Zoe."

Victor recognized the jerk standing in that doorway. How could he not? He'd been introduced to Xavier Winters and he'd even shook the guy's hand. A hand he'd wanted to break at the time. He'd held back, barely.

This is the bastard who hurt Zoe so badly. This is the guy who broke her heart.

Wasn't a broken hand the least the guy should expect in the way of payback?

"Tom?" Zoe took a step toward the other man, then stopped.

Tom strolled into the room, then paused to shut the door behind him. "Hello, Zoe. It's been a long time." He pulled a small black box from his coat pocket. "I like privacy," he said. "And while you both did pass the security search, I want to make absolutely sure that neither of you managed to smuggle in a listening device."

Victor didn't let his expression alter.

"There." Tom pressed a button on the box he held. "Now, we don't have to worry about anyone overhearing our conversation, do we?"

Audio jammer. Victor knew exactly what that little box was.

Tom paced toward Zoe. His gaze locked on her face. "How is it possible," he asked her, "that you've grown even more beautiful?"

The asshole was *not* flirting with her. Victor took an aggressive step toward the lawyer. "I didn't come here to talk to some middle man."

Very slowly, Tom's gaze left Zoe and drifted over to Victor. That faint smile — that annoyingly smug one — curved his lips. "Ah…so that's the way this scene was supposed to play out, hmmm? I have to confess, I was curious. Especially after I saw you talking with Roy at the police station. I wondered just what plan you might be spinning."

Victor's hands had clenched into fists. He hated this jerk. "You're not the kind of guy who gives orders. You take them. Just like you've been taking them from Luther Bates. How many years *have* you been on his payroll? Five? Six? I would've thought that you'd be tired of being Luther's errand boy by now."

Because he was watching so closely, Victor saw the way Tom's eyelids jerked at his jab. He'd figured a guy like Tom would have one big, overinflated ego, and an ego like that could be his downfall.

"Zoe…" Tom sighed out of her name. "I've tried to reach you many times over the years. Tried to talk to you again. I have so many regrets."

Oh, hell, no, the guy wasn't about to try to stir up that particular part of their past, was he?

Tom side-stepped so that he could stare at Zoe. "I've missed you."

She didn't say a word.

Victor focused on breathing, slowly and easily, and keeping his control. This little meeting was important. Too important to let his emotions rule. "I want to talk to your boss."

"I thought you just said my boss was Luther Bates," Tom murmured. "In case you didn't realize, he's still in prison. For the moment, anyway. If you want to talk with him, visit him there."

For the moment, anyway.

"I'm so curious about what plan you have going on here." Tom motioned toward them. "You bring her in here and—what? You act as if you're selling her out? That *is* what my client is accused of doing, correct? You think that Roy Duncan was going to trade Zoe for the two million dollar bounty that's on her head."

The guy was so damn controlled and cold. Emotion only flared in Tom when he looked directly at Zoe.

"He wasn't just doing it for the money," Zoe said, her voice husky. "A woman named Michelle Lane is missing. She was part of the deal. Roy said that if he brought me in, Michelle would be set free."

A faint furrow appeared between Tom's perfect brows. The guy's whole face was too sickeningly perfect. He needed a broken nose. Something to make him look more human. Victor would be happy to oblige the broken nose need.

"Michelle Lane?" Tom repeated as his brows furrowed even more. "Can't say I know that name. Why was she important for a trade? Is she a cop, too?"

Tread fucking carefully. Victor was afraid they'd already revealed too much.

"She was my friend. *Is* my friend," Zoe said, voice still soft. "And I want her back."

Tom laughed and the sound was bitter. Angry. "Oh, Zoe, you and I both know that you don't have real friends. You have people who want to use you. And you — because you are too damn *good* — you let us all do our worst."

She retreated a step.

"Take for instance…this man at your side." Disgust curled Tom's lips. "I imagine he's lied to you over and over, ever since the first moment he walked into your life."

Fucking hell.

"No." Her voice wasn't so soft any longer. "He hasn't. What he's done…Victor has saved my ass — over and over — since the first moment he walked into my life."

Tom's cheeks flushed. "He's worse than I am."

"No!" Now she was almost yelling. "Victor is nothing like you! Victor is good. He's a decent man who wants to help the world. He wants — "

"To use you." Tom spoke with devastating finality. "That's what he wanted from the moment he met you. Hell, even *before* you actually met. He'd been having secret meetings with your father for weeks. Did you know that? Did you know that Victor is the agent who has met privately with your father the most? He's the person who has visited Luther in prison *the most* since your father's incarceration."

Victor risked a quick glance at Zoe. She was shaking her head.

"Yes," Tom said. "It's true. An easy enough fact to check out—his visits are in the prison records. If you'd bothered to visit your father, you could have seen those records for yourself. But…" Now he walked toward the desk that waited on the right. He put the jammer down when he opened the desk. Pulled out a manila file. "I took the liberty of making copies for you during my last visit. Take a peek. Victor is Luther's most regular visitor."

She lurched toward the desk. Victor stood there, frozen, wondering just how much Tom could know—and how much damage the guy was about to do.

To Victor.

To Zoe.

To the trust that he'd worked so hard to build.

Zoe's hands were shaking when she reached for the file. But she didn't open it. Instead, she shoved it back across the table at Tom. "I don't need to see the records. Victor is an FBI agent. Of course, he visited Luther. He was working Luther's case when he first met me. He was—"

"Using you," Tom cut in sadly. "All along. He was using you, and you didn't see it."

She flinched.

"Shut the fuck up," Victor said, his voice low and deadly quiet.

"No." Tom didn't even glance his way. His focus was on Zoe. "I'm sorry this has happened to you — again — but you can't trust Victor. You don't know him. Not really. He's just some street kid who still belongs in the gutter. A punk who will use anyone and anything to get what he wants — "

Victor lunged for the guy. He shoved Tom back against the desk and drew back his fist, ready to strike.

But Tom laughed. "See what I mean?" he asked Zoe. "Is this what an FBI agent is really supposed to do? Or is this what a street fighter would do? A man who would fight anyone, anytime, if the price was right. A man who nearly killed one of his opponents." His gaze drifted to Victor's poised fist. "With his bare hands."

Zoe hurried toward them. Her fingers curled around Victor's arm. "Don't. I get that it's tempting. Trust me, I get it, but don't. I think the guy *wants* you to hit him."

Yeah, Victor suspected that. The problem was that he wanted to punch Tom, too. And if they both wanted it...

"I didn't fake how I felt," Tom suddenly burst out. "I never faked that. When I said I loved you, Zoe, that emotion was real."

Her fingers tightened on Victor's arm. "Let him go."

"I wanted to marry you," Tom continued, a bit of spittle flying from his mouth. *Not so controlled now.* "I didn't think you'd actually walk. I mean...who walks from that much power?"

"I do." Her simple reply.

Victor lowered his hand. He also let go of Tom and took a step back. The better to remove himself from temptation.

Zoe's chin lifted as she faced off against her ex-lover. "You see? Victor *is* the better man here. He's decent and kind and he wants to put the criminals *away*, not help them. He is nothing like you." She looked up at Victor, giving him that look that made him think...*Shit, she does trust me. She stares at me like I'm a good man.*

He felt like hell.

"Let's get out of here. He doesn't know anything about Michelle. Like you said, he's the middle man. He's not worth our time." She tugged on his hand and they headed toward the door.

They'd taken about five steps when...

"Elizabeth Ward." Tom said the name with relish.

Victor's spine stiffened.

"Does that name ring a bell for you, Zoe?" Tom pushed.

She glanced over her shoulder. "You know it does. When I was taken…the first damn time…she was there. Luther put a hit on Elizabeth. Her mother — she was his lawyer once, too. Only he had her killed." Her voice hardened as she warned, "Better watch yourself, Tom, because Luther doesn't have a good track record with attorneys."

And, once more, she started for the door.

"Elizabeth's mother was Luther's lover, too," Tom said.

She stumbled.

"You didn't know that, but your FBI agent, he did. He knew a lot. So many secrets…and he's been keeping them all from you."

She cast a quick, worried glance Victor's way.

He reached for the door. "Screw him, baby. It's time to go." Because this was *not* going down the way he needed. He strode into the hallway, pulling her with him. If they got a little farther away, that jammer wouldn't work any longer and his team would be able to pick up on the conversation again. Provided, of course, that the jammer had the short transmission distance he hoped…

"Victor knew." Tom had followed them. "Luther *told* me that Victor knew."

Zoe stopped in the middle of the narrow hallway. She turned to face Tom.

"Your FBI Special Agent knew that Luther was involved with that woman and even more—"

"Don't listen to him, Zoe," Victor interrupted, aware that he was sounding desperate. He had to refocus them all. Get the attention back on Michelle. The case. "The guy is a criminal. He's probably behind Michelle's abduction. I mean, shit, *he's* here, isn't he? And he was the one at the police station. How the hell did he even become Roy's attorney?"

"Victor knew—" Tom began and Victor couldn't hold back. He couldn't stop. There was *no* way he could let the guy say what would come next. Because maybe the listening device he wore *was* working again. And if Tom spilled this news, he would bring hell falling down on Elizabeth Ward.

So, before Tom could finish his sentence, Victor attacked. He lunged for the other man and this time, his fist flew. He drove his fist straight into Tom's jaw, a hard right hook that had—once upon a darker time—been his specialty. He wasn't particularly surprised to see that punch take Tom down. No way was the fancy suit meant to withstand hits like that.

While Tom lay on the floor, dazed, Victor grabbed the guy's shirt front and stood over him. "Watch the fuck what you say," he snarled.

"H-he doesn't want *you* to know…" Tom gasped out the words.

"Victor! Stop!" Zoe shouted. "Let him go!"

He heard the thunder of rushing footsteps and knew that Tom's guards were coming. Cursing, he let the bastard go and jumped to his feet. In the same move, Victor grabbed the listening device, one of his cuff links, and he crushed the damn thing in his fingertips. He couldn't let the other agents and cops hear—

"Elizabeth…is your…s-sister…and he *knew*."

Victor's gaze flew to Zoe's face. He saw her confusion, her shock, her denial, her…

Betrayal. Her eyes widened as she stared back at Victor. "He's lying." Her voice was almost ghostly.

The two guards were there. Big and Brawny—Samuel—made the mistake of swinging at Victor. He ducked the punch. Then Victor delivered one of his own—a hard hit to the guy's mid-section. The breath blew out of the fellow in a whoosh as the guard doubled-over.

The other guard—Kevin—had made the mistake of grabbing Zoe. She slammed her foot down on his shoe and drove back with her elbow. He swore and jerked her harder.

Big fucking mistake.

"Duck, Zoe," Victor ordered.

Her head dipped down and he used his right hook once more. This guy fell even faster than

Tom. Only he nearly took Zoe down with him. Victor grabbed her, held tight. Her body pressed flush to his. And she stared up at him once more with—

Betrayal.

"We're getting the hell out of here," Victor snapped. He'd fix this. He had to fix this.

"Is it true?"

He locked his fingers around her wrist and pulled her toward the elevator. "We have to go." Because the whole plan—it had been blown to hell. He needed to regroup. He needed to figure out why Luther would have told that information to Tom. Luther had been hell-bent on keeping the news of Elizabeth's paternity a secret.

Because if the truth got out, she'd have a two million dollar price tag on her head, too.

Not what he wanted to happen for his sister-in-law.

And that was why he'd smashed the listening device. No way could he allow that information to get out.

"Zoe!"

Fuck. Victor looked back. Tom was on his feet. His jaw was already bruising.

"Zoe! He's using you! Listen to me—*listen!* He realizes your father is close to getting out of prison, and he wants to stop that. He's under orders…do anything necessary to gain your trust. *Anything.* And this Michelle person…how do you know she isn't working with the FBI? That her supposed disappearance isn't all a scam?"

Victor jabbed the button for the elevator, but nothing happened. Hell. He needed the keycard. His hands closed around Zoe's shoulders. "Stay here."

"Is it true? Is she my sister?"

Yes. I am so fucking sorry, but...yes. "We'll talk later." When they were out of there. When she was safe.

She shook her head. "Why would you keep this from me?"

He spun away.

Tom had his sick smirk on his face. "Now she knows the truth about you."

Victor marched toward the guard who was still hunched over on the floor. "Keycard," he barked. "Keycard or I kick your ass right now."

The guy handed him a keycard.

But Tom stepped closer. That smirk stretched. "I have all of this on video." He pointed to the ceiling. To the small camera there. "You'll be arrested for assault."

Sonofabitch.

"I'll share the video and Elizabeth Ward...she'll become a target."

Victor stilled. Tom's voice had been so low that Victor knew Zoe hadn't overheard the dark threat.

"You'll be arrested, your precious career will go down the drain, and Elizabeth Ward will be dead. All of that *will* happen." Tom rubbed his bruised jaw. "Or you can make a deal with me. Right here. Right now." Again, his voice was too low for anyone else to hear.

But Victor risked a quick glance at Zoe. She stood in front of the elevator, her eyes wide, and her expression stark.

"You like deals, don't you?" Tom asked him.

He didn't make deals with the devil, not anymore. "What do you want?"

"Oh, I think that's pretty obvious." Tom's gaze slid over his shoulder. To the elevator. To Zoe.

"No," Victor growled as rage twisted in his gut.

"Yes." Tom nodded. "I want you to walk away from Zoe. She is *not* meant for you. You really think Luther would ever let you stay with his daughter? An FBI agent?" He laughed again, and the sound was mocking. "He'd kill you first."

Victor recognized the threat for exactly what it was — and he didn't give a shit. "I walk away, and she's dead. The price on her head — "

"I'll keep her safe."

"Victor!" Zoe called.

"You have until the elevator reaches the ground floor to make your decision," Tom told him, voice so soft and smug. "Because if you haven't chosen—and made the *right* choice by the time you reach the lobby—then your FBI and cop friends will be swarming...and they'll be coming to arrest you. One click on my computer, and the video of your assault on me—and Elizabeth's parentage news—will go far and wide. To the cops. To the FBI. To the Press. To all of Luther's enemies..."

Fuck, fuck, fuck. This bastard was smarter than Victor had suspected. "What the hell...if I'm already going down..." Victor began. But he didn't finish that sentence. Not yet. Instead, he swung his fist. And this time, hell, yes, he broke Tom's nose. Bones crunched and Tom howled in pain and fury. "Then I might as well enjoy myself a little more." He glared at the bastard—a bastard now clutching his broken nose. "That was for breaking her heart."

He whirled away and stalked toward the elevator. Toward Zoe. She watched him, her beautiful green eyes locked on his with every step that he took.

And as she stared at him, Victor saw the fear in her gaze. He'd never wanted her to look at him that way. Never wanted her doubt and her anger and her pain.

He stopped in front of her.

"Victor?"

There were a million things he needed to say to her. A million. But he had no idea where to begin. He lifted his hand and swiped that keycard so he could get in the elevator. So *they* could get in. He pushed her inside and turned to look back at Tom. Blood dripped down the guy's face and stained his suit. Tom glared at Victor with absolute hatred in his eyes.

The doors slowly slid closed.

CHAPTER FOURTEEN

The bastard had broken his nose. Tom swiped at the blood that kept gushing out and glared at the elevator. Victor Monroe was a pain in his ass. He was also a problem that *would* be eliminated.

One way or the other.

Tom swung around and stomped back to his office. He yelled at the guards. Those two had sure been freaking useless. If they failed him again, it would be the last mistake they made.

Tom headed toward his desk. He typed in the security code that unlocked the top drawer of his desk, and when he opened the drawer there, his laptop waited. He pulled it out, booted it up, and, a few keystrokes later, he connected with the building's security feed.

A couple more taps, and he was accessing the camera in the VIP elevator. He saw Zoe. Beautiful Zoe. She was still so perfect to him. All those curves. That husky voice. Those eyes that promised heaven. Perfect sex appeal. The arm candy he needed. The jewel that showed just how far he'd come.

And Victor Monroe was at her side. Looking furious. Desperate.

That's right. Be desperate. Because you don't have options, Victor. Soon, you won't have anything at all. No FBI. No freedom. No Zoe.

Tom had been prepared for this meeting. He'd gotten plenty of dirt to use from Luther and he'd even paid some folks at the FBI to spill the information they had on Elizabeth Ward. Oh, yes, he'd been ready.

At that moment, Victor's hand flew out. He hit the control panel once. Twice. He drove his fist into it again and again.

"What the hell?" Tom muttered. What was that freaking psycho agent doing? And, yeah, the guy was nuts. Based on the crazy shit he'd read in Victor's files, the special agent had more than a bit of a dark side going on. And Zoe thought *he* was the good guy?

When would she learn?

They truly were letting just anyone into the FBI these days. How disappointing.

Zoe tried to grab the guy's arm.

Tom's eyes narrowed as Victor swung toward Zoe, with his hand still fisted.

***

"What is wrong with you?" Zoe asked when Victor whirled toward her. His knuckles were bleeding. *Because the guy had just been pounding the hell out of that control panel.* "Stop it!"

"It is stopped." His hand fell to his side. She saw him flex his fingers. "I didn't have the right access to stop the thing the normal way, so I figured a couple of hits—if they were hard enough—might just do the trick."

Her heart was racing so hard that her chest hurt. It took her a frantic moment to realize what his words meant. Then she understood…*he'd stopped the elevator.*

"Now, to make sure *he* stops watching us." His head turned and Victor scanned the elevator. "Ah, there you are." He headed to the small, dark box positioned to the left of the elevator doors. The box was up high, but he could easily reach it. And he did. He smashed through the glass covering on the box, and shards of glass rained down on the floor. Then he yanked out the small camera. "Can't see us now, can you, bastard?" Victor broke the camera and tossed it away.

Her breath sawed in and out of her lungs. Her body was shaking. Fury and pain and fear twisted inside of her as she stared at Victor.

Sister. I have a sister and he never told me. She'd only met Elizabeth Ward one time. One desperate time. Then the woman had vanished. "You sent her away." The pieces were sliding into place, so very slowly now.

Blood dripped from his battered knuckles. "I was protecting her. Just like I've been protecting you." He stepped toward her.

She retreated fast, because she couldn't bear the idea of his touch, not right then. If he touched her, Zoe wasn't sure what she'd do. Break apart? Attack him? Maybe both? "Were you?" Her words felt hard even as they burst from her mouth. "Or were you just using me? Trying to isolate me even more so that I was completely dependent on you?"

"No." He shook his head. "No. I had to keep her safe. She married my brother—she's *family*."

"She's *my* family, too, dammit! I had a right to know!" Her eyes burned, but not with tears. Just...fury. Fury was all she could handle in that moment. She wouldn't let the fear and pain take over. She couldn't.

He was still shaking his head. "This isn't the place to talk about that, okay? I stopped the elevator, but that is just going to buy us a few minutes. Your bastard of an ex-lover will have his crews working to get this thing moving in no time." And he took another step toward her.

There was no place for her to go. She was trapped between him and the back wall of the elevator. His hands lifted—

"Don't," she ordered. "Do not touch me right now. I-I can't handle it, okay?"

He froze.

"My heart hurts," she whispered. But the words were a lie. Her heart didn't just hurt. It felt as if it had been ripped right out of her chest. Tom had been telling the truth. Victor's reaction left no doubt about it. Elizabeth Ward was her sister. Victor had known and kept that secret from her. And if he'd kept that secret...*how many other secrets does he have?* "Why did you do this to me?"

His jaw locked. His face held no expression—his features were just tense, but his eyes blazed with desperate emotion. "You knew, all along, that I was working your father's case. I *told* you. You knew I had a job to do. You even said you realized I was—"

"Why did you have to make me fall in love with you?" There. She'd said it. The stark, horrible words were out and she couldn't pull them back. Zoe didn't want them back. "Were you following orders? Doing *anything* to make me trust you?" She had to swallow twice in order to keep speaking. "Was that what your boss at the FBI ordered? My trust...so you could control me?"

"Zoe..." The desperation flared even more in his eyes. "I never wanted to hurt you."

Sometimes, it was what people *didn't* say that mattered the most. She'd just told him that she loved him. And he'd said…

I never wanted to hurt you.

Those words hurt the most. They told her that while she'd been giving him her heart, while she'd been getting lost in him, Victor had just been following his orders.

Building trust.

Breaking her.

"You kept holding back," he rasped. "No one could get through to you. We knew Luther was working some new plan. We can't let him back on the streets. He was supposed to cooperate with us — that was the whole reason you had protection."

Her heart hurt even more. She lost her breath. *The whole reason.* Right. Because when Victor was with her, it wasn't personal. All business. How could she have ever forgotten that?

"He can bring down nearly the entire East Coast crime syndicate — and the guy can destroy Vegas, too, you know it. His ties are that fucking far reaching. But he stopped talking — he went back on the deal we'd made."

A deal that had been set up to protect her. "I guess I didn't mean that much to him. Not when his own freedom was on the line."

Victor reached for her once more.

"No!"

His hands slammed down on either side of her head, his palms hitting the mirrored back wall of the elevator. "We don't have time."

He kept saying that crap.

"Tom is trying to take you."

"Get away from me, Victor." She hurt too much. He was too close. She couldn't *think*.

"He offered me a deal. Dammit, it's a deal I don't want to take."

Now she laughed, bitterly. "But you're the man always making deals."

"*Tom wants you.*"

"And you don't." No, hell, she hadn't meant—

"I want you more than I have ever wanted anyone or anything in this world." Victor's words were guttural. "Never doubt that. You are not just a job. I am an asshole, a cold-hearted bastard. A fucking fool. And you are the best thing that has ever come into my life."

Now she was the one to shake her head. She wouldn't believe him, not again. How many more lies did he have to tell?

"Your trust is gone. I saw it happen. I saw it die in your eyes. I saw the moment when you started to look at me the same way everyone else does." His breath was ragged. "I didn't want that. Not with you."

The elevator jerked. He swore.

Being so close to him was too painful. "Let me go."

"Baby, please…listen to me."

She didn't want to listen. Was it so wrong that she wanted to lick her wounds? "Michelle." Saying the other woman's name helped to stiffen her spine. "She's what matters now. We have to find her. We—"

"Tom knows where she is. That guy is in this mess up to his eyes."

Yes, she was afraid he was.

"But I can't take him down. If I fight him right now, he's going to expose Elizabeth. She'll be a target. Do you want hitmen hunting her, the way they are you?"

No. No, she didn't. "I wouldn't wish my life on anyone." Being Luther's daughter was its own brand of hell.

The elevator jerked again. "Tom wants you," Victor said again, the words so dark and rough. "And if he doesn't get you, when this elevator stops, I'll be charged with assault."

"Then maybe you shouldn't have attacked the guy!"

"I know! Shit, *I know!* But he knew my weakness. Going in, he fucking knew…knew about Elizabeth. Knew that I would attack to try and keep him quiet. He used that. He planned that whole scene up there. We were here, looking for the bastard who has been pulling all the strings, looking for the man who was going to swap Michelle for you, and I think we found him."

"Tom?" Tom had always been low on the totem pole. Not a power player in her father's organization. Hadn't that been why he'd wanted to marry her?

Once more, the elevator lurched. Only this time, it didn't stop with that jerk. It began to descend.

"I have to walk away," Victor said. "It has to *look* as if I'm walking away."

"I don't understand." He was leaving her now?

"If I go to jail, I can't protect you. If he releases what he knows about Elizabeth…she's next on the kill list."

They were almost at the lobby level. Above the elevator doors, she could see the shining lights counting them down.

"He'll take you."

What?

"It's part of the deal. I am so fucking sorry."

"You're…leaving me?" How could the pain keep getting worse?

"When this elevator gets to the ground floor, I have to walk away. But I am coming fucking back. There's no way I'm giving you up."

Walking away…it sure sounded as if he were giving her up. "I was a case."

"No." Hard, rough. "You are everything. Remember that. To me, you are *everything*. Fuck the case. Fuck the FBI. Fuck Luther Bates."

The elevator dinged. The doors opened.

"You are everything."

Then he kissed her. A deep, hard, desperate kiss. One that made her ache for the things that they'd had. For what *could* have been. She wanted to wrap her arms around him and hold tight but she didn't move.

Well…didn't move except for the tear that slipped from her eye and slid down her cheek.

"Boss wants to know…" A nasally voice grated. "You make your choice?"

Victor's head lifted. He looked over his shoulder. She saw the two men standing just past those open elevator doors. More guards with ear pieces.

"She's my choice," Victor said. He turned back to stare at Zoe. "She always will be." He put his forehead against hers. "I am so damn sorry. I wish I could start over again. I'd do everything differently with you. *Everything*."

The guard said, "Boss is going to—"

Victor let her go. He whirled to confront the guards. "Tell your boss we aren't done. When it comes to Zoe, I'm never done."

Then he strode forward. The guards slid away, opening a space for him to pass.

And he just…

Left her.

Left her standing in that elevator. Left her all alone.

Zoe pressed her lips together so that they wouldn't tremble, and she tasted him. She could still feel him. Even though he was…gone.

Gone, without a second glance back.

She straightened her shoulders. Marched forward, but the guards didn't let her pass.

They blocked her way. "Boss wants you back upstairs."

"I don't really give a shit what he wants."

One of the guys grabbed her arm, tightly, in a grip that bruised. "Funny, we don't really give a shit what *you* want, either."

The other guard jammed a gun into her side. "You're going back upstairs."

"Victor!" she yelled.

He stopped.

The guards pushed her deeper into the elevator.

Victor had swung around to face her. She saw the fury and the pain on his face. So much emotion, but he wasn't moving toward her.

"Victor," she whispered.

"Those earrings are fucking gorgeous on you."

The elevator doors closed.

CHAPTER FIFTEEN

He'd never wanted to destroy someone so completely. Victor stood in the casino lobby, people all around him, the whir of slot machines and the too high peal of laughter grating in his ears.

She loves me, and I have so fucked everything to hell and back.

His hands were clenched. Every muscle in his body was poised to attack.

Zoe had been afraid when she called out to him. He'd heard the terror in her voice. She'd been afraid, and he'd been helpless to do anything to save her.

Someone bumped into him. A hard hit in his shoulder. "Sorry, buddy," the guy muttered and kept going.

Not just a stranger—Cain, doing his undercover work. Scoping out the casino. Victor whirled and grabbed him before Cain could go too far.

"Watch where the fuck you're going!" Victor yelled at him. Then he jerked Cain closer.

"Penthouse. Tom Winters has Zoe up there. I need eyes on her." He shoved the guy away. Glared.

Cain glared back, but, knowing how to play his part perfectly, he whirled away, muttering about "Drunk assholes" as he headed toward the elevator bank.

Victor heaved out a hard breath. He tried to figure out his next move. Tried to think past the desperation and fear choking him. Then…his head turned. He found the security camera perched high on one of the white columns that lined the lobby.

Tom would be monitoring him through the casino's cameras. Watching his every move. Victor stared into that round lens a moment. Then he said, quite clearly, moving his lips slowly so he could be sure that Tom would understand. "Zoe. Is. Mine. Hurt her…and you die."

Then he headed out of the casino. As soon as he cleared those big, gleaming entrance doors, he yanked out his phone. He was going to have to move, hell fast. He dialed his brother — the man he *thought* of as his brother. Saxon Black. The guy who'd been at his side when they were desperate teens on the street. The man who'd followed him to the FBI when Victor had wanted to stop *being* a criminal and to fight against the bad guys out there. The agent who'd lost his heart to Elizabeth

Ward…and who'd gotten out of the FBI because he'd wanted a normal life, with his new love.

The phone rang once, twice. Then…

"Vic? Hey, bro, long time, no talk," Saxon greeted.

"Elizabeth may be compromised. Get her the fuck out of the country right now."

Silence. Painful. Stark.

"Get her out," Victor snapped. "Get a burner phone. When you're someplace safe, call me to check in."

"Vic…what's happening?"

He turned back to stare up at the glittering lights of the Vine. "I fucked up. All those secrets I keep? The ones you warned me about? They're coming back to bite me in the ass now." And they were biting hard.

"How can I help?"

That was Saxon. That was his family. "Help by protecting Elizabeth. That woman is carrying my niece, and I damn well want them safe." Another fucking secret. One that he hadn't been able to tell Zoe.

Zoe, baby…I will make this up to you. I will find a way.

"We'll be gone within the hour."

Victor knew Saxon would do anything necessary to protect Elizabeth and the baby.

He ended the call. Kept walking. The street was full of traffic and Christmas lights and people laughing with their freaking holiday cheer. His world was imploding and everyone else just carried along with their business as if *nothing* was happening.

He needed help. So much help. Russell and new agent Lauren McDaniel were waiting around the corner in an unmarked van. They'd expect a full report from him, but a full report was the last thing he could deliver. And the local cops working this case — they were already seething. That seething would just get worse. One of their own was missing, and he had no new information to give them on Michelle's whereabouts.

He pressed another button on his phone. Sometimes, the FBI and the cops couldn't help. Sometimes, the only people who could help were your family. He waited, with the phone pressed to his ear, until the call was answered.

"Victor…" Jasmine's voice was soft, worried. "What do you need?"

I need Zoe back. "Help," he managed. "I need you and Drake to help me." Because he was about to cross too many lines. He was about to break the law. About to turn his back on the agency. About to do anything necessary…to protect Zoe. To keep his unborn niece and her mother Elizabeth safe.

To stop Tom Winters.

To stop Luther Bates.

To get Zoe back with me.

***

The gun stayed in Zoe's side during the elevator ride. It pressed harder to her as the guards escorted her down the narrow hallway and toward the penthouse. One goon opened the door for her and pushed her inside.

Tom was leaning over his laptop when she entered the room. He looked up at her and a wide smile split his face. "You came back to me!"

"At gunpoint," she responded. Her hand rose and pressed to her right earring. She sure hoped she was activating the device the right way. Victor had told her to just press down on the little diamond stud…Zoe tried to make the move just look like a nervous gesture.

Those earrings are fucking gorgeous on you. She'd gotten Victor's message, loud and clear. Now she just hoped—*I can get Tom to confess to me.*

Tom motioned dismissively toward her guards. "Leave us."

That was it? *Leave us?* No reprimand for the guns? The guards scurried out, shutting the door behind them.

Tom's nose was swollen. Dried blood was on his face. And his jaw was bruised a deep purple. Hardly the suave man that she remembered.

"I'm sorry that I had to be the one to tell you the truth about Victor Monroe." Now Tom sounded sympathetic. Was she supposed to buy that bull? He wasn't sympathetic. He was like Luther—psychopathic.

"You have to be more careful who you trust," Tom added.

She had to be more careful? Her vision seemed to go red as she stalked toward him. Fury drove her. A fury that left her ice cold.

His smile widened as she approached. The fool looked so confident and smug. Time to change that. Time to change everything.

"Victor doesn't matter." She could lie easily. After all, she was her father's daughter. Zoe smiled at Tom. "Not at all." Her right hand slid toward the top of her dress. The neckline dipped, exposing the upper curves of her breasts. Tom's gaze followed the movement of her hands and his breath hitched faster.

Men. So disgustingly predictable sometimes.

She leaned closer to him. Her fingers skimmed inside the vee of her dress, reaching just under the bra that she wore and—

In a flash, she'd pulled out the small knife that Victor had given to her. Her first present from him. A very handy gift. She shoved that knife right up against Tom's throat. He instantly went still.

"I am so sick and tired of being used," she whispered to him.

His Adam's apple bobbed. "I-I can understand that."

Her eyes turned to slits as she stared up at him. "Michelle Lane."

"I don't—"

She let the blade cut his skin. A fat drop of blood trickled down his neck. She wanted to show the guy she meant business.

But…

He laughed. "You aren't going to kill me. We both know that. You may be Luther's daughter, but you don't have his…instincts, shall we say?"

Why did people always underestimate her? "Don't be too sure of that. Right now, it's taking every bit of self-control I have not to slit your throat from ear to ear."

His laughter stopped. Maybe he believed her. Maybe he didn't. If he pushed her more, they'd both find out whether or not she was bluffing. "You went to see Roy at the station. How did you become his lawyer?"

"We have an…acquaintance in common."

"Michelle?"

He didn't speak.

So the knife cut deeper.

"You have her," Zoe said. "*You're* the one in charge here. The one using this big ass fancy office."

"I have come up in the world since we last met," he allowed.

"Is she alive?" Zoe had to know.

"Move the knife, and I'll tell you."

"Is she alive? Dammit, it's just us in here! Why keep lying to me? Why keep—"

"She's alive," Tom said. His face changed. Went cold. Sinister. "And she'll stay that way, as long as you keep cooperating with me."

Ice spread from her belly to her lungs...to her heart.

"If you want Michelle Lane back, well, *you* have to work a deal with me."

Disgusted, her lips curled at him. "Why is everyone all about deals these days?"

His hand flew up and closed around her wrist. She tensed, locking down to make sure he couldn't jerk her hand—and her knife—away from his throat.

"What can I say?" Tom murmured. "I guess folks like a good deal."

Bastard.

"You're the only one who can do this particular job. Do it...and all the hits on you will vanish. The slate will be clean. Michelle will be released, and you won't have to look over your shoulder any longer, always worried about the next attack."

He was so wrong. "There is no way for me to escape."

"I've been working both sides." His thumb stroked the inside of her wrist. A sensual movement. She had a knife to his throat and the asshole was acting as if they were about to make out.

In his freaking dreams.

"You suspected that, though, didn't you, sweetheart?" Tom murmured. "I saw the suspicion in your eyes when you saw me walk into this room."

"My father treated you like shit years ago. I didn't buy that you were suddenly jumping to do his bidding again."

"No." Again, he stroked her wrist, right over her racing pulse. "But he doesn't understand how I feel about him. He thinks I'll keep doing his dirty work forever, but times have changed. While he's been locked up, I've had access to his contacts. I *used* them. I created my own empire."

"And you're the new power in Vegas."

He inclined his head toward her, not seeming to care that when he moved, the knife cut even deeper into him.

"I'll be even more powerful once you do one simple task for me."

She was staring at a monster. "You're the one who put the two million dollars on my head."

He shrugged.

"You did it."

"Guilty."

Her fingers trembled with the effort of holding back. *Cut his throat. Cut it.* Maybe she was more like Luther than she'd realized.

"I didn't think you'd actually *die*, you know." Now Tom sounded offended. "It was only two million, after all. The heavy hitters don't really get involved in business like this—you know, with a guy like Luther Bates hanging in the background, poised for epic retaliation—unless it's at least four million."

Insane bastard. "You put a hit on my life."

He gave a little shrug. "I moved the pieces on the chess board."

She could see herself killing him. In that moment, it would be so easy. One slice. Done. Sure, the blood would pour on her and he'd probably fight as he went down...

The same way my mother had fought. The same way the blood had pumped from her. The same way...

"You've gone so pale, sweetheart. I'm sorry, but, come on, at this point in your life, shouldn't you just expect betrayals?" Then he twisted the wrist he'd been stroking. Hard and brutally and the bone snapped.

She didn't cry out, but the knife she'd held slipped from her fingers.

"I had to put the hit on you. I didn't know where you were hiding. I needed you to come out. To come back to me. It's the same reason I took Michelle. You had to come to me…and you did."

"I could've died, asshole!" Her wrist throbbed. The pain was so intense that nausea rose within her and dizziness had her swaying. "If it weren't for Victor—"

"Ah. Dear Victor. He's the man I knew would save you. After all, you are his weakness. I'd long suspected that, and it was so nice to get the confirmation from Roy. Roy would have told me anything—everything—of course, because the fool actually thinks I'm going to help him." His head leaned toward her, right next to her ear, as if he were sharing a special secret when he whispered, "I'm not. I'm going to let him go to jail and I'll let one of the prisoners kill him there. Just like I sent another prisoner to kill that fool who tried to shoot you in the alley."

"*You* sent that shooter!"

"And I couldn't risk him turning on me." He spoke with no emotion. "Just so you know, I *did* include a bonus in the hit…a bonus that would be paid if you were brought in alive. See? I was doing my part to protect you, too."

What? That was insane.

"I needed you back, Zoe."

"Why me?" Why was she so important?

"Because, sweetheart, you're the only one who can do this special job. The only one *he* won't see coming." His breath blew over the shell of her ear. "If you want Michelle back alive, if you want *your* life back — no hits, no enemies, nothing but you dancing your heart out on a glittering Vegas stage, *my* stage — then you just have to do one thing for me."

"What?"

He eased back so that he could stare into her eyes. Then he smiled as he told her, "You have to kill Luther Bates."

***

Victor yanked open the side door of the van.

"Hell, yes!" Russell said as his fist shot into the air. He had headphones on and was leaning over a computer. Lauren sat at his side, her eyes gleaming, and a wide smile on her face.

"We just got the bastard," Lauren whispered. *"We got him!"*

Victor shook his head, not understanding.

"Zoe activated her listening device as soon as she got close to Tom," Russell said. "We recorded every single word that prick just said to her. We got his full confession. That bastard is going *down*."

She'd done it.

"He's the one who took Michelle," Lauren said quickly, shoving back her hair. "He's the one who put out the hit on Zoe. He's the one who's been doing it all." She gave a quick, excited laugh. "Your plan worked freaking perfectly."

His plan? No, no, it hadn't worked out so well. If it had worked out, he'd still be up there. He'd be keeping her safe. "Is she all right?" Victor asked and he heard the desperation in his own voice.

"She's still talking," Russell assured him quickly. "That means she's still alive. He's going to keep her that way. The guy has a job for her."

"What job?"

Russell and Lauren shared a long look. Lauren's laughter was gone. "He wants Zoe to kill her father," she said quietly.

"Give me the fucking headphones."

Russell nearly threw them at Victor. He put them on and heard Zoe's voice, seeming to flow right around him.

***

"Kill…Luther?" Zoe laughed at Tom. "You must be out of your mind. He's in a maximum security prison."

Tom wasn't laughing. "That sweet little knife you just pulled out of your dress? You can smuggle one just like it into the prison. I'll make sure the guards don't search you too thoroughly. Luther will let you get close to him. Hell, pretend you're giving the guy a hug. Then slice his throat open."

"No."

"Come on, Zoe…" Now his voice was low, wheedling. As if the jerk hadn't just broken her wrist. "You know you want some payback. How fitting would it be…especially after what he did to your mom."

"Stop." She didn't want to hear this. She didn't want the people listening to hear this. She just needed it all to stop.

"You were there. I know you were. Luther told me…said it was the one part he regretted. Not killing her, of course, but that you saw it. He said you even tried to stop him. To save her."

She could feel her mother's blood on her fingers. On her clothes.

"He tells me things…because I'm his lawyer. Because he knows that I can't do anything with the crimes he reports. Confidentiality and all that. Lawyer and client privilege."

"No." Her chin notched up. "He tells you because you're just as sick and twisted as he is and you don't care what he's done."

Tom's face hardened. "I'm giving you the opportunity for payback. You should be thanking me."

Had he always been crazy?

"Don't you think it's fitting that you be the one to take him out? And only you can do it. You can get close enough. He's on guard with everyone else. Go in there, kill him…and get your life back."

"If I kill Luther, then I'll be the one in prison! I'll be rotting behind bars!"

Tom snorted. "For killing Luther Bates? Hardly. I'll be your lawyer," he promised. "I'll get you off. All I have to do is tell the jury about your mother. About the poor teenage girl who was found clinging to her mother's dead body because she couldn't let her mom go. The girl who has a history of mental and physical abuse at her father's hands. They'll pull jury nullification. No one will convict you, no matter what evidence is there. You will walk, I guarantee it."

***

Her mother. Dear God, her mother… Victor had suspected this truth, but hearing the story this way cut him up. He could barely breathe because he hurt so much…for her. All for her.

Zoe had been through too much in her life. All that pain and she still smiled. Still looked for the good in the world. In people.

In me.

He wanted to take her far away from any pain and betrayal. He wanted to make sure that she was happy for the rest of her life. That she was always smiling. Always happy. Always…

With me.

But she probably wanted to get as far from him, as fast as she could.

"We have the confession we needed." He yanked off the head phones. He stood facing the van, his eyes on the other two agents. "Now we have to get her out of there."

"No." The voice was sharp and it came from directly behind him. "No, Special Agent Monroe, that is *not* how this operation will go down."

Victor turned — very slowly — and came face-to-face with FBI Assistant Director Percy Chase. The guy wore a long trench coat and his shoulders hunched forward as he glared at Victor.

"There is a police officer still missing! Or have you forgotten that?" Percy blasted at him. "If we move now, we may never see that woman again."

"I haven't forgotten a damn thing, and if we move now," Victor gritted right back, "we can force Tom to tell us where Michelle Lane is. We have the power and the fucking confession, thanks to Zoe. Now we need to do our part and get Zoe out of the Vine before she gets hurt."

When he'd left her in that elevator, he'd known that she would be able to get Tom's confession. Zoe was smart and tough and strong. She humbled him with her goodness. She made him want to change the whole world for her. She made him—

I love her.

"Once we know where Michelle Lane is, then we move." Percy was adamant. "Not a minute sooner. It's not like Tom Winters is going to kill Zoe. I was listening, too."

Of course, he fucking was. That had been one of the reasons Victor hadn't wanted the truth about Elizabeth to leak. He'd known Percy was out there on surveillance watch, too. There had been far too many ears listening.

"He needs Zoe," Percy said. "He won't kill her."

"If she doesn't do what he wants, then Tom *will* hurt her. He could be hurting her right now." He couldn't stand the thought. "Shit, the man took out a hit on her! Doesn't that tell you he isn't exactly sane? If he's pushed, if he gets angry with her, he'll spiral out of control. Zoe—"

"Can survive a little pain." Percy waved his hand dismissively. "This case is huge. It will go down in the books—make my career *and yours.* You hear what I'm saying? When we do this…the right way…you can have any job at the Bureau that you want. We're going to have Tom Winters for all the crimes he committed, and we'll have a new murder to pin on Luther Bates. Bates will tell us everything we need to know about the crime syndicate in the East. We will destroy them all."

There was silence from behind Victor. He could feel Russell and Lauren watching him.

"And all of that…" Percy murmured. "All of that can't really be measured against a bit of pain that one woman might experience for a just a little while, now, can it?"

Victor studied the assistant director. Tall, thin, balding. An arrogant, cold bastard.

"Tell me what you want," Percy continued, swallowing a bit nervously as the silence stretched and Victor kept glaring at him. "Name your title, tell me the job, just tell me what you want because you have more than earned everything—"

"I want Zoe."

Percy's face hardened. The streetlight overhead glared down on him. "She'll be fine, once we've finished the case. When we know where Michelle Lane is being kept, when we have the police officer in custody, then you can take Zoe back into protective custody." He rubbed his hand along the back of his neck. "Though I'm thinking that it will be time for us to turn her over to Witness Protection. She gives us what we want on Bates, and then we set her up in a nice house somewhere in the country."

"I'm not giving her up." Cold, lethal words.

"She's just a case," Percy responded flatly. "You, of all people, should know that personal involvement is never a good idea. I have to say,

I'm mighty disappointed in you. Here I am, offering you the world and you—"

"She is my world." And she didn't know it.

A long, black limo turned onto the street. When he saw that limo, Victor knew that Drake and Jasmine had arrived. Talk about fast back-up. Drake had told him they were close, but Victor hadn't realized just how soon they'd be on the scene.

"Get your head in the game, Agent," Percy snapped. "Stop thinking with your dick."

Victor stepped toe-to-toe with the bastard. "This is my last case. I've been planning a career change for a while now."

Percy's jaw dropped. "*What?*"

"I'm going private. My brother-in-law and I…we'll be doing some ventures together." He gave the assistant director a cold smile. "So consider this my notice, asshole. I'm done with you and your shit. And if you *ever* say anything that so much as *feels* a little negative in regard to Zoe again, I will beat the ever loving shit out of you. FBI or no FBI."

"B-but—but—"

"Now, I'm going in the Vine, and I'm getting Zoe out. I'm doing that shit, either with your support or without it." He narrowed his eyes on Percy. "You're a dumbass who hasn't been in the field in over ten years. You don't know when a situation is about to go super nova, but I do, and I *won't* risk her."

Percy puffed out his chest. "I won't allow a single other agent to follow you in there —"

"*This* agent will be following him in," Russell announced as he jumped out of the van. "Because Victor Monroe has never steered me wrong. I'll cover his back."

Percy sucked in a sharp, stunned breath.

"I've been meaning to say," Victor murmured to Russell. "I could sure use you in my new business venture."

"We'll talk about my split soon enough," Russell assured him. "Count on it."

Victor nodded. It was good to have the right friends at your side.

Drake and Jasmine were closing in. Russell was ready to go. And Percy...

"Get the fuck out of my way," Victor barked at the guy.

The assistant director stumbled back.

***

Lauren knew she had just been witness to a scene that would become legendary at the FBI. Victor and Russell had just handed the assistant director his own ass.

Now they were striding toward the Vine, and Percy was just standing there, looking lost. No doubt, he was feeling lost, too.

She cleared her throat. The idea of striding after those guys was tempting, but she'd just started her career with the FBI. Walking away now? Not so much an option for her.

But doing the right thing? That was what they should all do. "Sir," Lauren began carefully as she climbed out of the van and moved toward him, "we have Tom's confession. The longer that we leave Zoe Peters with him, the more volatile the situation will become."

He whirled toward her. "You think I need some rookie telling me how to do my job?"

Her chin notched up. "Right now, yes, sir, I do." *Try another tactic.* "Unless you want Agent Monroe getting *all* of the credit for the takedown. I mean, if you are providing tactical support, the operation is still technically under your supervision. But if you let him go in there, without any of *your* team…well, you're essentially turning everything over to him."

His jaw hardened. "You were a fucking psych major in college, weren't you?"

"Yes, sir." She actually had a Master's in psychology.

"You think I don't know when I'm being played?"

"I think you don't know how to be human." There. She was probably going to get some really shitty assignments in the future, but she'd spoken the truth. "Didn't you see the way Victor looked when he talked about Zoe? He loves her. And you were asking him to just keep risking her life. That wasn't going to happen."

"Victor Monroe doesn't love anyone."

She bit her lower lip. Maybe the assistant director needed to take a few psych classes.

"He doesn't," Percy said stubbornly.

"Then why did he just quit the FBI so that he could rush into the Vine and get Zoe Peters back to safety?"

"The cop needs us!"

On that, she agreed. "Then the FBI should be pulling out all the stops. We save Michelle Lane *and* Zoe. We storm that place and we don't let anyone get in our way." Each word came out more heated than the last. "I didn't join the Bureau to sit on the sidelines. With respect, sir, I joined to kick some ass."

He was silent a moment.

Her hand nervously tapped against her holster. Every moment that passed was a moment that everything could be going to hell inside of the Vine. Every moment…

"Agent McDaniel," Percy barked. "Get the tactical team moving."

"Right away!" A wide grin split her face. She rushed to follow his order.

"And Agent McDaniel…"

She looked back.

"I think I like you." He nodded. "You'll go far at the FBI."

"Good…because that's just what *I* want."

CHAPTER SIXTEEN

"So what's the plan?" Jasmine demanded as soon as they headed toward the casino.

The plan? *Get Zoe. Keep her safe always. Throw Tom Winters in a cell and never let him see the light of day again.*

He took the gun that Russell offered to him and tucked it in his waistband. "The plan is for me to distract Tom Winters." A simple, basic plan. "I'll get all the attention focused on me. While I do that, Jasmine and Drake, you two find a way to access the Vine's security files." Jasmine had always been gifted with computers. "You get on the network. Get access to every secret you can find."

Russell gave a low whistle. "You think you can find Michelle Lane by hacking the place?"

"It's sure as shit worth a try. Get control of the system," Victor ordered them. Drake and Jasmine both had plenty of talents — many of which weren't exactly legal. "I want you to take control of all the security cameras. Turn off the feeds." Now his gaze zeroed in on Russell. "As soon as they have control, you get up to the penthouse because I will be needing your backup." He had no idea how many guards would come running once he attacked. "We arrest Winters while we still have our FBI badges and we get Zoe the hell out of there." He glanced at the team, trying to make sure everyone was in agreement with his spur-of-the-moment plan. *It's better than nothing.*

Drake nodded. "Sounds good to me…provided you don't get yourself killed while you're fighting to get the guy's *attention.*"

Jasmine grabbed Victor's arm. "He won't." The threat was in her eyes. "He'd better not."

"Don't worry, Jazz. I've got too much to live for now. Dying isn't on my agenda."

Her brow furrowed. "Vic?"

"I need her. I can be happy…with her." *I am happy with her. As long as I can get Zoe to forgive me. As long as I haven't screwed things up too badly. As long as I have a chance.*

Jasmine's face softened. "Then let's get her the hell out of that building."

Damn straight.

***

"I need proof that Michelle is alive." Zoe licked her lips. They'd gone desert dry. Her wrist still throbbed and nausea churned in her belly. "Before I do *anything* else, I need proof."

Tom tilted his head to the side, seeming to consider the matter.

"Proof of life," Zoe whispered. "I have to get it or there is no deal that will ever happen."

"Fine." He marched back to his laptop. Typed on a few keys. Then he spun the laptop around to face her. "Here you go."

She inched closer to the desk so that she could see the laptop screen. Video footage was playing. Footage that showed a woman—bound hand and foot and gagged—as she lay on a lush, four-poster bed.

"I gave her a nice suite," Tom said. "Pity she can't really appreciate it."

Michelle is in the hotel.

"Now…" He snapped the laptop closed. "Do we have a deal?"

"I can't kill Luther Bates."

He sighed. "Fine." Tom pulled out his phone, dialed quickly, then put the phone to his ear. "The guest in room 2804 is checking out. Make sure there isn't a mess when she leaves."

The guest…

"No!" Zoe screamed because she knew exactly what the bastard was doing.

"No?" Tom's brows climbed. "Why not? Michelle is of no use to me if you won't make the deal for her. Better to just kill her now."

"No, don't!"

"Then do we have a deal?" he asked silkily. "Say it, Zoe. I need the words. I need to hear you say that you'll kill your father."

"Why?" Zoe paced away from him, hurrying toward the windows that overlooked the city. She'd gotten his confession. When Victor had spoken those last words to her in the lobby, she'd realized what her job was. She'd *done* the job. Now shouldn't the FBI be storming in to save the day? Tom had just said where Michelle was. She'd seen her…*alive.* It was time for the good guys to swoop in and stop this nightmare.

Only…no one was swooping. Her shoulders hunched as she stared at the street below. There was no sign of swarming cop cars. No men and women in bullet proof vests rushing toward the building. "Why do you need me to say the words?" Zoe asked, trying to buy some more time. "So you can record me…the way you recorded Victor's little attack on you? Then you'll take my words and show them to Luther. Show him that I could never *really* be trusted. That you're the only one who had his back all this time." She was just bullshitting but even as she said the words, they did make a twisted kind of sense. Frowning now, she glanced over her shoulder at him. "*Why* do you want me to say the words?"

His eyes gleamed. "You've always protected him."

No, she hadn't.

"Luther told me that you were the one who would never turn on him, no matter what. That blood was thicker than anything else."

Zoe shivered. "And he wasn't going to promote you in the organization because you weren't family." *Not unless you married me.*

"Screw that old family mob nonsense. I have the brains. I know this operation inside and out."

You don't know me.

"I want to hear the words because it will make me fucking happy to hear them. Consider it my final payback against him. He was always so sure you'd keep choosing him. That you'd never do anything against him." Tom laughed. "Even when you were screwing the FBI agent, Luther was adamant that you could be trusted. That you wouldn't reveal anything that would hurt him. And the damn thing is…you haven't. You were in FBI custody for months and you still didn't talk. No new charges came against Luther, and every day, he just got cockier and cockier."

There was still no one storming the penthouse. There was only silence, all around her.

"You've got so many damn weird daddy issues," Tom spat at her.

And she had to laugh. "Yes, I do." A cold smile curved her lips. "But you want to know why I never talked? Why I didn't go to the FBI?" She lifted her hand to her right ear. Pressed on that little earring. To him, it would probably just look like another nervous gesture. To her…

I'm turning off the feed.

She thrust back her shoulders. "I didn't talk because I'm not some innocent girl. I never have been."

He was watching her with curiosity gleaming in his eyes.

"I saw him kill my mother, but that wasn't the only time I saw who Luther truly was. He made it his mission for me to see everything. To know *everything*." All of the pain she'd held in check bubbled out now. "He planned for *me* to take over his operation, you see. So he forced me to watch the blood and the pain and the hell he wrecked. I didn't get sent to boarding school right away. I stayed with him. He made sure of it. And sometimes…" Her voice grew raspy. "He made me help him."

Tom's eyes had widened.

"One day, he brought in a drug dealer who'd tried to betray him. Luther wanted me to take care of the guy. Me. A teenager. When I told him that he was crazy, Luther put a gun in my hand." She was shaking as she remembered this. "He put a gun in my hand and then…then he put *his* gun to my head." She lifted her left hand, made it into a pretend gun, and put it right next to her temple.

Shock covered Tom's face. *I guess Luther didn't tell you this secret.*

"Luther said either I would kill that guy or I would be the one dying."

Tom took a few fast steps toward her. "*You* killed the dealer. That's why Luther was so certain of you. He had that man's death on you. So if you betrayed him, then he'd turn you over to the cops—"

"I didn't kill him."

He stilled.

"The guy was crying, begging in front of me. Saying he'd made a mistake. That he'd never do it again. Luther was yelling for me to shoot. And I—I yanked the gun up. I turned it on Luther and I shot."

Tom blinked. "You...shot Luther?"

"And he shot me." Her breath sawed out. She moved her hand, brushed back the heavy mane of her hair, and showed him the faint white scar on the side of her head. She worked to constantly hide that scar. Even Victor had never seen it. "Because I'd moved, the bullet...it didn't do much damage to me. Just grazed me. *My* bullet tore into Luther's stomach, but he had doctors at his beck and call. They fixed him right up."

"What happened to the drug dealer?"

Her gaze lowered to the floor. "When Luther was better, he brought me to see the man again. And he made me watch while the guy was slowly tortured. It took five days before he died. By that point, I wanted to kill the guy just to stop his pain."

"Luther has always been good at getting what he wants." There was *admiration* in his tone.

There was only hate in her voice as she said, "When it was over, Luther told me that it was all my fault. Every cry. Every scream. Because things could have ended quickly for the guy. But they didn't. Because I did that. I made him hurt more. And Luther told me that if I ever tried to stop him again, he would make sure *everyone* I cared about went through that same hell." She let her hair fall. "Once you see someone die that way…while you are helpless to stop their pain…it changes you."

He came toward her. Lifted her hair again and traced that faint scar. His touch revolted her, but she didn't move as he said, "Luther shot his own daughter."

That was the part that she thought Luther might have regretted. Because when their guns had exploded that faithful day, and blood had poured down the side of her head, Luther had screamed. Not with fury. Not with pain.

With fear.

And he'd screamed her name.

Tom was silent a moment, then he shrugged as he dropped his hand. "I still want to hear you say that you'll kill Luther Bates."

"Fine." She bit off the word. "I will kill Luther Bates. Are you happy now?"

"I'm—"

The doors to the penthouse flew open. No, they'd been *kicked* open. Chunks of wood flew through the air. Victor stood there, chest heaving, a gun in his hand and fury on his face. "Guess what, asshole?" he shouted at Tom. "I decided I didn't fucking like your deal." He reached into his pocket and yanked out the keycard he'd used in the elevator earlier. He tossed it onto the floor at Tom's feet. "So I'm making a new deal. One that involves me, walking out of here with Zoe. And you—you spending the rest of your life behind bars."

Tom rushed toward his desk. He yanked open his laptop and started tapping on the keys. "You shouldn't be up here! My guards should never have let you—"

"The guards I encountered on my way up are...indisposed, so to speak." Victor flashed his shark's smile. Definitely killer.

"The video feed isn't coming up!" Tom yelled. Spittle flew from his mouth. "What in the hell?"

"Oh, must be a technical glitch," Victor said, sounding not even a little surprised. "That shit happens."

Tom's hand dropped away from the laptop.

"Zoe…" Victor said her name softly. Carefully. "Zoe, why are you holding your wrist that way?"

And she realized she was cradling her right wrist against her stomach. "It's broken."

Victor's face…changed. His eyes seemed to burn brighter, but his expression became so dark, so menacing that, for a moment, she almost felt as if she were staring at a stranger.

"Come here, Zoe," Victor said softly. He still had his gun aimed at Tom. "Come to me."

Right. This was it. The good guy swooping in. Only she wasn't convinced Victor was the good guy, not any longer.

I hate secrets. I'm so sick of them. Sick to death of them. She started walking toward Victor. At least this particular nightmare was over.

"Stop, Zoe." Tom's voice was mild. "Take another step, and the guard in Michelle's room will blow her brains out."

Her gaze jerked to him. His fingers were poised over his phone.

"One click, and I send the order to kill. Maybe my security system is glitching, but I can still use my phone and text just fine. The guard in the room will kill her, and Michelle's blood will be on you. Just like your father said…everyone you care about, right? It goes back to you. To *your* fucking choices."

She stilled.

"Come to *me,* Zoe," Tom said.

"Zoe…" Victor growled.

"To me or she dies." His finger was so close to the phone's screen.

Zoe looked at Victor. "Tell me that the FBI heard which room she's in. Tell me that a team already has her and that he's bullshitting me. Please, please…*tell me that.*"

A muscle flexed in Victor's jaw. His gaze was still locked on Tom. "Drop the phone or I will shoot your ass right now."

That is Victor's answer. He wants Tom to drop the phone because Michelle isn't safe yet. The FBI doesn't have her. But Tom's finger was too close. If Victor fired, Tom could still carry out his dark order. He could hit send on the text—

She rushed toward Tom. "Don't."

With his left hand, Tom grabbed her, yanked her close and used her as a human shield. "You have got to stop caring so much about other people. Serious weakness, sweetheart."

She didn't think so. Caring about other people—that was what stopped her from becoming a monster. From being just like Luther.

He'd wanted her to stop caring. He'd wanted to alienate her. To make her see that people couldn't be trusted. That your friends turned on you. That your lovers betrayed you.

Only blood matters.

She stared across the room and into Victor's eyes. He still had his weapon up and aimed. Only right then, it was aimed at her because in order to shoot Tom, Victor would have to shoot her, too.

"How the fuck do you really think this will end?" Victor asked as he eased closer. His grip on that gun never wavered. "Here's a newsflash for you, *Tom*. Zoe was wired. The FBI heard every single word you said up here with her. That jammer on your desk—you turned that shit off when I left, remember? Only you forgot to turn it back on. We've got you. You are done."

"No!" Tom's hold on Zoe tightened. "No, I won't go down like this! I won't!" And she knew he was going to send that text. She couldn't let it happen. Zoe threw her entire body back against Tom and they fell to the floor in a heap.

***

"I've got her," Jasmine said as she looked up from the computer monitor. The techs who'd *been* working in that room were unconscious at Drake's feet. "The cop is being held in room 2804." Her gaze darted over to the wall of monitors on the right. The security footage still showed on that wall, but the feed wasn't going to

Tom Winters, not any longer. She'd fixed that jackass.

"Looks like the rest of the cavalry is coming in," Drake said as he, too, looked at the monitors.

The FBI was swarming through the building's front doors.

Jasmine leapt to her feet. "Let's get to Michelle before someone panics." She'd seen that happen before. With the authorities bursting in, people would get desperate. And a desperate person could become trigger happy at the wrong time.

But...

She looked at the top monitor. A monitor that showed the penthouse. The penthouse...Victor was up there. And she knew he was not going to leave that place without Zoe.

"Kick ass, Vic," Jasmine muttered, then she turned and ran for the door. They had a cop to save.

***

Cain Blair crept down the hotel hallway. He'd kept his ear piece in place, and he'd heard every damn word that Tom Winters had said to Zoe.

Victor had told him to haul ass up to the penthouse and give Zoe back-up, but there'd been no way for him to use the VIP elevator. He hadn't had access so he'd gone as high as he could on the hotel's regular elevators, then he'd started climbing stairs to get his ass in the proper attack position.

Only…before he'd made it to the penthouse and to Zoe, he'd heard Tom spill Michelle's location. He'd known exactly what the dick was talking about when he said it was time for the guest in room 2804 to check out.

So instead of hitting the penthouse, Cain was now on floor twenty-eight. He was getting Michelle out of there. He was going to make sure she survived. He could see the guard standing in front of the door to room 2804. The guy was big, muscled, and he *would* be going down.

Cain whistled as he approached the guy, trying to look as if he belonged—

The guy grabbed him. "No one should be this close to the suite! No one should—"

Cain head-butted the fellow. "And you should sure be friendlier to strangers." In a flash, he had the guy cuffed and on the floor. "Stay there."

"You bastard! You—"

His yells were going to alert any guards inside the hotel room. With no time to hesitate, Cain slammed his shoulder into the door. Only it didn't give. Shit—that was a hard door. So he slammed again, hitting harder, football style, and the door gave way. He rushed inside.

A guard was already coming at him, gun up.

"Las Vegas PD!" Cain shouted. "Drop the gun, now!"

The guy didn't drop his weapon. "I hate cops!"

Shit. The fellow was firing. So Cain fired, too. His gun exploded and the bullet hit the guard's shoulder, sending him flying back. Cain lunged forward, he kicked the gun out of the way and told the downed man, "Move again and the next shot will be in your heart."

The guy—finally showing some sense—stopped moving.

"And you're damn lucky your bullet missed me. Asshole." Cain's gaze jerked around the room. He saw Michelle, twisting and straining against her bonds on the bed. She was alive. Hell, yes, she was safe.

He took a step toward her.

And felt the muzzle of a gun shove into his back.

"Not just one of us in here, cop," a rough voice barked behind him. "Should have searched better…"

Not one guard inside. *Two.* Shit.

"Now you drop the weapon," the second guard told him. "Or I will shoot you straight in your spine."

The spine? Damn. Someone sure played dirty.

Good thing I do, too.

CHAPTER SEVENTEEN

"Bitch!" Tom shouted as he punched at Zoe. He hit her in the gut, a blow that sent the breath heaving from her, but she hit him back even harder. A twisting jab that went right for his balls.

He howled and eased his grip on her. Before she could go in for another hit, Victor was there. He yanked her away from Tom and pulled her to her feet. His gaze swept desperately over her.

"I'm fine, I'm *fine* – "

He pushed her behind him and faced Tom. Tom was staggering to his feet. Yelling and cursing and charging at Victor.

Victor raised his gun. Pointed it straight at Tom's head.

Tom froze. The gun was less than an inch away from him.

"Want to see what kind of damage a shot this close can do?" Victor asked him.

Tom's gaze darted to Zoe. "She knows…" he said.

She fought the urge to slam her fist into his balls — again.

"You're about to know," Victor promised him.

Tom lifted his arms. "You can't shoot when a guy isn't fighting you, *Special Agent*."

"Technically, I've turned in my resignation," Victor said. "So maybe I'll just call this self-defense. Justified. I'll make the world a better place by taking you out of it."

Zoe shook her head. No, Victor couldn't do that. If he did, if he crossed that particular line, there would be no going back.

Not for him.

Not for her.

Footsteps pounded in the hallway. She looked over her shoulder and saw Russell hurrying into the room. He was armed and his expression said he was ready to face hell.

But he drew up short at the sight of Victor holding his gun on Tom. "Guess you got things covered, huh?"

"Back-up is always appreciated," Victor assured him. "Always."

Tom's lips curled in disgust.

"Michelle!" Zoe looked around the room, desperate. "Do we know if she's okay? Is she safe? Russell, *do you know what is happening with Michelle?*"

***

Cain dropped his weapon, but the bastard behind him just jabbed the gun harder into his back.

The guy taunted, "Guess what, cop? Weapon or not, you're still getting that shot in the back. You're still—"

There was a quick thud of sound. A grunt. And the gun was suddenly *not* jabbing into Cain's spine any longer. He spun around and found a blond man—a tough looking asshole who wore a fancy suit—and a gorgeous woman with cold and deadly eyes staring at him.

"We thought you could use some assistance," the woman said.

The guy flexed his fingers. Cain realized that the stranger had knocked out the guard who'd been ready to shoot—*right in my freaking spine.* "Guess that means you're the good guys?" Cain asked carefully. The blond fellow looked familiar…

Drake Archer. The name clicked for him. Though Archer wasn't exactly known for being good.

"Today, we are," Archer said. "Victor sent us."

Okay, that was good enough for him. Cain turned away from them and hurried toward the bed. Michelle was twisting and fighting her ropes and grunting frantically behind her gag. He yanked off her blindfold and saw her dark eyes flare. He pulled down her gag. "Michelle, it's okay, you're safe—"

"Zoe!" Michelle yelled the name.

"Zoe is going to be okay," Drake said. "Victor is taking care of her."

Cain yanked at the rope that bound her wrists. "You don't—don't understand." Her body trembled. "He's obsessed—he's…he's not letting her g-go…"

"Yes, he will." The woman at Drake's side spoke with certainty. "Because Victor isn't going to give that bastard a choice."

A tear leaked down Michelle's cheek. "I think…I think he'll kill her…before he lets her go again…He'll kill Zoe…"

***

Zoe was safe. Zoe was alive.

Zoe is with me. Victor's heart was still racing, fear still hollowing out his stomach, but Zoe was okay. He'd gotten to her. Stopped Tom. And Michelle should be safe. Jasmine and Drake would never let him down.

While Russell kept his gun pointed at Tom, Victor pulled out his phone. He pressed the buttons to connect him with Jasmine and while the phone rang, he waited, nervous as all hell. *I need confirmation that Michelle is still alive.*

"We've got her," Jasmine said when she answered the call. "Michelle is safe, and just so you know, the FBI cavalry is storming the building right now."

So Percy had finally decided to do the right thing. A little late to the party, but that was the assistant director's normal style.

"But Vic...watch your ass up there, okay?" Worry thickened Jasmine's voice. "Michelle is saying that Tom is freaking obsessed with Zoe. That he never got over her — that he's been pulling all of these strings and setting everything up so that she had to come back to him."

Victor's gaze slid back to Tom. The guy didn't look like a threat any longer. His shoulders were hunched. His body still.

"And if he's spent all this time working toward the goal of getting her back," Jasmine continued, her words rushing out, "then how will he react when you take her away?"

"I don't give a shit how he reacts. There's nothing he can do. Zoe is safe, and he's about to spend the rest of *his* life behind bars."

At Victor's rough words, Tom's head jerked up. Fury burned in his gaze.

"Thanks, Jazz," Victor said. "I owe you." He put the phone back in his pocket. Zoe was still

beside him, still cradling her broken wrist.
Fucking asshole.

And she was still…
Not looking me in the eye.

He'd deal with that. Deal with her—later. As
soon as they were out of that building, he'd start
fixing things with her. He'd beg. He'd plead.
He'd move heaven and earth, but he *would* fix
things. There was no alternative for him.

He needed her too much.

Russell had cuffed the guy. He shoved Tom
forward and tossed a pleased glance at Victor.
"Not too bad for our last case, huh, Victor?"
Russell asked.

Not too bad, but not too good, either, because
he'd screwed things so completely with Zoe.

"You can't trust him," Tom said, his attention
focused on Zoe. "You know that, right? Don't
ever trust him. He'll just keep betraying you. Just
keep using you."

"Shut the hell up," Victor ordered.

But Tom continued, voice heating as he said,
"He doesn't care about you, Zoe. He never did.
He's been using you all along. Don't fall into that
trap again."

"*Shut up!*" Victor's roar blasted through the
penthouse.

"He doesn't care—"

"I know he doesn't." Zoe's soft words cut
right through Tom's rage-filled rant. "I know."

And then she did finally look into Victor's eyes. The sadness and pain he saw in her green stare ripped through him. "But at least he came back." Her lips twisted in a sad smile. "So thank you for that Victor."

"Zoe—"

But she'd already turned away from him. She stared at Tom and shook her head. "I don't think prison will be kind to you. Luther…he has a lot of connections inside prison walls. When people realize *you* betrayed him, what do you think they'll do to you in there?"

Tom paled. "No…"

"Maybe you should make a deal," she said as she turned away and began walking toward the door. "You and Victor…you're both good at deals."

Victor felt those words pierce his heart.

Tom was watching her leave, a wistful, almost sad expression on his face. "Good-bye, my Zoe."

"I was never yours." She kept walking. "Never anyone's. I'm my own person. So screw off."

Tom's gaze hardened.

She kept going.

Victor wanted to run after her. He had the feeling he'd be spending the rest of his life doing that. Rushing after her. Hadn't that been their story all along? She slipped away. He found her.

And this time, I beg her to forgive me.

"I've got this joker," Russell said, his voice sympathetic. "Do what you need to do, Vic."

But, once more, Victor's gaze jerked toward Tom. There was still sadness on his face, but something else was there, too.

Triumph?

Why would the guy be all triumphant now? Michelle was alive. *He* was cuffed. What the hell did Tom have to be celebrating? Not a single thing unless…

How will he react when you take her away? Jasmine's words played in his mind again. Frowning, he said, "You put all of those hits on Zoe."

Tom just kept staring after her.

"She could have died at any time. If I hadn't been there, she *would* be dead."

Tom's gaze finally slid toward him. "Too bad you aren't there now, huh, Special Agent?"

What?

Triumph blazed like insanity in Tom's eyes.

Then Victor understood. *This isn't over.* Victor ran for the door, bellowing Zoe's name.

She was standing in front of the elevator, her head bowed. At his shout, she jerked and looked up at him. "I don't have the stupid keycard. I can't get it to open."

Fuck the keycard. "Tom has a hit on you!"

Her lips twisted. "He only wanted to get me to the hotel. It's over."

It's not. Victor pushed faster, determined to get to her. And he yanked at his holster, pulling out his gun. "Zoe!"

"It's. Over."

The elevator doors dinged.

Someone had just come *up* to the penthouse. "Zoe!"

The doors opened and gunfire thundered. Her body flew back and Victor saw the blood — Zoe's blood. The guard came out of the elevator. Samuel. The jerk he'd fought earlier. The guy came out, with his gun still raised because Zoe was still alive.

"Boss said...you don't leave," the guard growled. "You never leave him. Extra pay for that..."

And Victor knew that Tom had never intended to let Zoe escape that hotel. When she'd walked inside...

Either she'd be Tom's or she'd be dead.

"No!" Victor fired, again and again and the guard was the one to jerk back as the bullets hit him. They flew into his chest, sank into his heart and the bastard fell, slamming back into the elevator.

Victor rushed to Zoe. She had her hands on her stomach and the blood was pumping out, soaking her fingers. She stared up at him, her face slack with shock even as her eyes filled with fear. "Vic...tor?"

"You're okay." There wasn't any other option. "Do you hear me? You're okay." He put his hands on her wound.

Russell rushed out, hauling Tom with him. "Victor!"

"It hurts," Zoe whispered. "More than when Luther shot me..."

More than when...*Fuck.* "Look at me, Zoe!" Because her eyes had sagged shut. Her body had slumped against the wall. "*Look at me!*"

Her eyelids flickered as she looked up at him.

"You should have stayed with me," Tom called, voice so cold. "Then you would have been safe. I told you, Zoe, the special agent wasn't really the good guy. If he had been, you wouldn't be dying right now."

Victor ignored him. He stared at Zoe. Gorgeous, strong, perfect Zoe. "You're okay."

Her lips trembled. "I'm...not..."

Russell was on his phone, calling for help. Demanding that paramedics get to the penthouse right away.

"You just...you have to get stitched up." Her blood soaked his hands now. *Zoe's blood is on me. I should have kept her safe. Should have seen this threat coming.* "Then you'll be as good as—"

"Love...you..."

"What?"

"Now...l-lie...to me..."

"Zoe—"

"Lie to me..." Tears leaked from her eyes. "Say...you care. Say—"

"Zoe, I love you!" The words ripped from him. "Do you hear me? *I love you.* I've been in love with you for so long—hell, even before the first time you ditched your guards and escaped. *I love you.*"

Her eyes were closing again. "Good...liar..."

"No!" He couldn't just watch her die. He picked her up in his arms, held her tight and raced into the elevator. He kicked the guard's body out of his way so that the damn doors would shut. "I'm not lying." He pressed the button for the lobby. "I love you. Love you so much that I've been a blind idiot. You are my world, Zoe." The doors closed. The elevator shot down to the lobby. "You are everything that matters to me, and you are *okay.*"

Her face had bleached of all color. "Such...liar..."

"Baby..." It wasn't a lie. The love he felt for her was ripping him apart. Tearing, destroying, killing...

As surely as the bullet was killing her.

No! I can't lose her! I won't. "Fight, Zoe. Stay alive. Stay strong. *Stay with me.*"

The elevator doors opened. He ran into the lobby and saw—

The assistant director. Lauren McDaniel. Cain. Jasmine. Drake. Other agents. Uniformed cops. They all stared at him in shock. "An ambulance!" Victor yelled at them. "Get me an ambulance!" Because...

She's not okay. Zoe is dying. I can't let her die. Please, God, don't let her die.

He ran for the big, shining doors that led out of the Vine. Jasmine was with him, racing at his side. The others just gaped. Pity was in their eyes.

As if...as if Zoe was already gone.

She was limp in his arms, but she wasn't gone. Not yet. Not Zoe.

"I love you," he whispered again.

But Zoe didn't respond.

"I love you." He would say it a thousand times. A million. He needed her to understand. She wasn't just a case. She was Zoe. She had his heart. She had his soul. She owned every single part of him.

He heard the shriek of an ambulance's siren.

"I love you," Victor whispered again. He stood there, Zoe in his arms, her body too still, and he felt tears on his own cheeks. "Don't leave, baby. Stay. I'll give you anything you want...*just stay.*"

The ambulance roared to a stop in front of him. The attendants rushed out. They took Zoe from him.

"Victor…" Jasmine reached for his arm. "Victor, I am so sorry."

He climbed into the ambulance. The EMTs were frantically working on Zoe. She wasn't responding. "I love you," he told her again.

Someone slammed the doors shut.

"I love you," Victor whispered to Zoe.

CHAPTER EIGHTEEN

Five days later…

Victor Monroe stared through the thick jail bars, his gaze on his prey — Xavier Thomas Winters. The lawyer wore a garish orange prisoner uniform, stubble lined his jaw, and the nose that Victor had broken — it was still swollen and twisted.

Not so perfect now, are you?

But the guy was smiling. That smug-ass smile that Victor hated.

"How's my Zoe doing?" Tom asked him.

Victor didn't blink.

Tom's fingers curled around the bars. "The story I've heard is that she didn't even make it to the hospital. She died on the way there." His lips twisted. "Such a shame. Why didn't you protect her better, Special Agent Monroe?"

"I'm not a special agent any longer."

Tom blinked. "You're not…here for a deal?"

"There won't be any deals with you. You're exactly where you belong — and exactly where you'll stay…until you die."

Tom's smug look was long gone.

"How long do you think you have?" Victor mused. "Before a hit is taken out on you?"

Tom licked his lips. "I have a...lot of information...on Luther...on—"

"Luther's prison is my next stop. I have to go break the news to him about his daughter. Tell me, how do you think he'll react? To knowing that *you* ordered the kill?"

Tom's breath hitched, coming faster and faster. "I wasn't going to let her leave again. I got her back. Worked too hard. *She wasn't going to leave again.* You knew the deal. You were supposed to walk away. She stayed. That was the arrangement. She *stayed.*"

Victor glanced around the small cell. "And now you'll stay here. Have fun." He turned on his heel and headed for the exit.

"Wait!"

He kept walking.

And Tom started laughing. "You...loved her, didn't you? Sonofabitch...I see it now. You weren't just using her. You're so fucked up in the head because she's gone. You're broken. The big, bad agent. All lost because Zoe is *gone.*"

Victor looked back at him. "You loved her, too."

That stopped Tom's laughter.

"And *you* broke when she left you. That's how you became this sick thing that I see now. You couldn't handle life without her."

"I was getting her back…"

"You became the same monster she'd always hated." Victor's lips curled in disgust. "Know this, though. At the end, Zoe loved *me*. Me. Despite everything, she still loved me." He flexed his fingers. "And I will always love her." He exhaled slowly. "Enjoy life behind bars. You deserve every bit of hell that you have coming." Once more, he started walking toward the exit — and toward the uniformed guard who waited there.

"I want to make a deal!" Tom shouted.

Victor motioned for the guard to open the door.

"Did you hear me? I want a deal! I'll talk! Give me a deal! Get me out of here!"

The guard opened the door.

"I want a deal!"

"Too fucking bad," Victor said without looking back. "Because I already told you, I don't deal with the devil. Not anymore."

He left that cell. Marched outside and wasn't particularly surprised to find two familiar cops waiting for him. Cain Blair and Michelle Lane. Michelle still had bruises on her body, leftover reminders of her time with Tom. Victor was sure that was she was itching for some alone time — and payback — with the guy.

Cain stared at him, pity in his eyes. Victor had been getting that look a lot lately. His heart ached every single time he saw it.

Cain strode toward him and offered Victor his hand. "I'm sorry it didn't end…differently."

Victor didn't speak. He just nodded as he took the guy's hand.

"I hear you're opening a private firm. Good luck with that, man," Cain told him quietly. "If there's ever anything I can do for you, just say the word."

The guy was a good cop. Solid. "Thank you."

Cain stepped back. And Michelle…a tear slid down her cheek. "She was my friend," she said, her voice husky. "Did she know that? Did she realize it? Zoe wasn't just a case. She was always more to me. She *cared* about me." Her breath hitched. "She was my *friend.*"

That ache in Victor's chest grew worse as he stared into her tear-filled eyes.

"Tell me…" Michelle begged. "Please tell me that at the end…she knew. I don't want her to have died, thinking — "

Victor swallowed. "She knew. She knew the truth about us both." He hoped that Zoe had known when she was fighting to live and her blood was pumping out so quickly. "We loved her."

Michelle nodded. Then she threw her arms around him, holding him tightly. "I'm so sorry that she's gone."

"Me, too." He didn't move within her embrace. He couldn't. Pain held him in check. The pain in his heart—a heart that would never be the same after Zoe. "Me…too."

***

Two days later…

Luther Bates.

Mob boss. Criminal mastermind. Prisoner.

Victor sat across the table from the famed killer, a cold knot heavy around his heart. He stared into Luther's eyes…the eyes of Zoe's father.

He hated the bastard.

"Is it true?" Luther asked him, tilting his head. "Is my Zoe dead?"

Victor stared back at him. After a long moment, he said, "Is it true…you once tried to kill *my* Zoe?"

Luther's eyelids flickered.

Hold onto your control. Victor mentally counted to ten, then said, "Xavier Thomas Winters is the man who ordered the hit on Zoe. He's the same man who wanted Zoe to come in this prison and slit your throat…the same way that you slit the throat of Zoe's mother." Beneath the table, his hands were tight fists. Zoe had been dealt so much pain in her life.

She'd deserved joy. She'd deserved freedom.

She'd gotten screwed by everyone. Used too much. Hurt too often.

I am sorry, Zoe.

"Did Zoe tell you about that?" Luther's voice had gone low, ragged. Before Victor could respond, Luther leaned forward. He rested his cuffed hands on the table. "I try not to think about that day. She was going to leave me…going to take Zoe away. Never let me see my blood again."

Like that would have been a bad thing.

"I've done plenty of dark things in my life. But Zoe…no matter what I did…no matter what I did to *her,* she stayed good." Luther's bound hands slammed onto the table top. "My one good thing." He hit the table again, harder. "My one good thing." Again, a hit hard enough to make the table top crack. *"My. One. Good. Thing."*

The prison guard stepped forward, but Victor waved him away. "You should cooperate with the FBI now."

Luther's hands spread out over the cracked table.

"Cooperate with them," Victor said. "A new agent, Lauren McDaniel, will be taking over your case. Tell her what she needs to know. You owe the FBI that much."

Luther's head snapped back. "A new agent? Where the hell are you going?"

"Someplace else. Someplace far the hell away."

Luther's gaze swept over his face. "You look like shit."

"Huh. Yeah, I feel that way, too." He forced his hands to unclench. Zoe's face flashed in his mind's eye. "She wasn't just good. Zoe was perfect." *Too perfect for me, but I still wanted her.*

"Heard you were there…at the end."

Victor assessed Luther and said, "You hear a whole lot for a man living behind bars."

"Tom Winters will pay for what he did." A faint smile tilted Luther's lips. "Perhaps he's paying right now."

Victor stiffened. Was the guy saying he'd already ordered Tom's death?

"I disgust you," Luther said, still with his head cocked as he studied Victor. "Yet you…loved her? My daughter?"

I will always love her. "Zoe was nothing like you."

Luther's gaze dropped to the table. "No," his voice was soft. Sad. "She was like her mother."

"The woman *you* killed, in front of Zoe. You sick fuck. Zoe deserved so much better. She should have been happy. She shouldn't have been hunted. She should have been living her life any way she wanted. With a safe home. With a family that loved her. With *everything* she wanted."

Luther wasn't looking at him. "We both knew she'd never have that while she lived. My daughter couldn't."

The hair on the nape of Victor's neck rose. "Your daughter is dead, and we are done. You will never be seeing me again." He pushed to his feet and stared down at Luther Bates.

Slowly, Luther looked up at him. Were the guy's eyes wet? No way. No damn way. Not this guy—the guy who'd made Zoe's life hell. Luther was a psychopath. He didn't—

"Thank you," Luther whispered.

Victor didn't say another word. He turned on his heel. Walked out of that prison. Kept walking until he was at his car. He never let his expression alter. He cranked the car, curled his hands around the steering wheel, and drove away.

Zoe…

***

Three days later…

Victor closed the suite door. He could hear the roar of the ocean. The waves were beating against the beach down below. The cold chill of Vegas was long gone. Hawaii was warm. Beautiful.

A perfect escape.

"I was wondering when you'd show up…"

He looked up—and into the most beautiful green eyes that he'd ever seen. Zoe stood in front of the open balcony doors. Her arms were at her sides, and a blue cast covered her right wrist. Her face was still too pale for his liking, but she was so gorgeous. The most perfect thing he'd ever seen.

And she was *alive*. Despite what so many others thought…Zoe had survived, and now she was free. He'd had to be so careful getting to her. He hadn't been able to leave when she was flown out of Vegas—flown on Drake's private plane with Drake's own physician, a guy who'd been paid extremely well to forget Zoe's existence.

Victor had tied up all the loose ends. Made sure that the world believed Zoe was gone.

After all, he knew how to make a person vanish. He'd done it before.

"Victor?" Zoe frowned at him. "Are you all right?"

He leaned back against the door. No, he wasn't all right. Because she *had* nearly died, and he'd almost lost her. "I wasn't sure you'd be here. You have a habit of running away."

She laughed and that sweet sound made the ice melt from his heart. "Who runs from paradise?"

He wanted to run to *her*. To wrap his arms around her and hold her tight. But he'd screwed things so completely with her. He had to make amends. He would spend the rest of his life making everything perfect for her. "I'm sorry."

Her expression was guarded. "For what, exactly?"

"Lying." He took a tentative step toward her. "Keeping secrets." Another step. "Not being good enough for you." Because he knew that he never would be.

A furrow appeared between her brows.

"But most of all…" Another step. She hadn't backed away, thank Christ. "I'm mostly sorry that I didn't tell you I loved you sooner. Because, Zoe, I do love you. I love you so much. I—"

"I know." Again, her voice was soft. "I heard you…" Her left hand rose and brushed lightly over her stomach. Over the wound that he knew was still covered in stitches. "I heard you talking to me in the ambulance."

He could almost touch her, but fear held him back. "There's something you need to know." Before anything else happened, he had to tell her this part. He'd sworn to never keep another secret from her again. "It's about Luther."

He saw her tense.

"I think…I think he may suspect that you're still alive."

"Why?" Fear broke in her voice. "What makes you say that?"

"The way he responded." *We both knew she'd never have that while she lived. My daughter couldn't.* Luther's words kept replaying in his head. "But Luther isn't going to say anything. He *wants* the world to think you're dead. That way, no more hits will ever be put on you. You're safe now. You can have any life that you want."

"Can I?" There was doubt on her face.

"Yes." He'd make sure she got her dreams. Every one of them.

"The problem is," she murmured. "I don't know just what life I *do* want now."

Victor knew what he wanted. He was staring at her. "Is it too late?"

"Too late for what?"

"Us." The one word was ragged. "Too late for us to have a chance. A future. Because, Zoe, that's what I want. All I want. To be with you. To make you happy. To have you look at me—" But he broke off.

Zoe inched closer to him. "To look at you...how?"

"With trust in your eyes. With love. To look at me...and see someone *worth* loving."

"Victor..."

She was going to tell him no. "Please." He was begging her. He'd never begged for anything. Only for her. Always for her. "I can make this right. I can do anything you want. I can—"

A knock sounded on the door.

Zoe tensed.

"It's okay," he told her quickly. "It's just…" He turned away and hurried toward the door. "It's just for you." Victor opened the door.

Saxon Black stood on the threshold. Saxon — his chosen brother. Tall and strong and with one serious go-to-hell edge, Saxon had been his friend on the streets and then his partner at the FBI. But Saxon wasn't alone. He'd brought his wife Elizabeth with him.

Elizabeth…*Zoe's half-sister.* And Elizabeth was very obviously pregnant.

"Zoe…" Victor cleared his throat. "There is someone you need to officially meet." Time to start eliminating all of the secrets. Time to make amends. "Zoe, this is your half-sister, Elizabeth."

There was dazed shock in both women's eyes as they stared at each other.

And…

Beneath the shock…there was more. Recognition.

Hope?

Zoe offered her left hand to Elizabeth. Her fingers trembled.

"Victor…" Saxon began, his voice rough and angry.

"Secrets just destroy," Victor said. "So let me see if the truth can help everyone to heal."

***

She wasn't alone any longer.

Zoe stood on the balcony, her gaze on the beach below. Elizabeth was gone, but her half-sister had assured her that she would be back, very soon.

Elizabeth was her family. The baby that Elizabeth carried — a little girl — she would be Zoe's niece.

I'm not alone.

The pain she'd felt for days had finally faded. Her heart was beating so fast, and a smile wouldn't leave her face. She knew life wasn't going to be perfect. Nothing was ever perfect. But...things were better.

For the first time since her mother had died, Zoe thought about the days that would come with hope.

Footsteps shuffled behind her. She didn't look over her shoulder. She knew Victor was there. Silent, strong Victor.

Victor...who said that he loved her.

"You shouldn't overdo," he told her carefully. "Your doctor said that you had to rest and recover."

Her hand curled around the wooden balcony. "I'm not overdoing."

"You're not thinking about jumping over that balcony and running, are you?" He moved closer to her. His words only sounded as if he were half-kidding.

She considered the idea of running and found…no, she didn't want to run. She wanted to stay exactly where she was. "Will I be getting a new home here in Hawaii?"

"Yes. As soon as you're feeling stronger, I'll take you out and we'll find the perfect place."

The perfect place for her…or them? "Where will you be?" She turned to look at him. "Heading off on another case?"

Victor shook his head. Night had fallen, and a thousand stars glittered over them. "I'm done with the FBI. I'm starting my own business, and I can run it from any location I want."

"So where do you want to be?"

His hand lifted and his fingers skimmed down her cheek. "I want to be where you are."

Her heartbeat drummed even faster.

"I would trade everything I have to take away the pain I caused you," he whispered as he stared down at her. "I want to make you happy. I want to prove myself to you. I want you to love me again."

To love him again? "Victor…" She shook her head.

His hand fell away. He stepped back. She could *feel* his pain in that instant. "I'm sorry," he whispered. "So fucking sorry." He turned away.

She grabbed his arm. "I never stopped loving you. That isn't how it works."

He looked back. "Zoe?"

"I love you. *I love you*, but if you ever keep another secret from me again, I will totally make your life an utter living hell, do you understand me?"

"You love me?"

"Do you understand me?" Zoe jabbed his chest. "Because you don't keep secrets from the people you love. You share everything. Good. Bad. The stuff in the middle. That's what you do when you make a life with someone."

"I want to make a life with you." His words fired out in a rush. "I want everything…with you."

She smiled up at him. During her time on the island, she'd been able to do a whole lot of thinking. And she'd realized…

I want Victor with me.

"I love you," he told her, voice so rough and dark. "I always will."

She stopped jabbing his chest and instead, her fingers curled around his shoulder. "And I will always love you." She rose onto her toes and kissed him. Not a wild and passionate kiss.

Softer. Sweeter.

A kiss that made her whole body feel warm. Feel safe. Feel…

Loved.

Victor Monroe. Ex-FBI bad-ass. Ex-street fighter. All around trouble.

And he was hers.

That hope in her heart blossomed even more. Yes, she really couldn't wait to see what tomorrow would bring...what would happen in the days ahead.

Because the new life that was waiting? It was hers. Her life with Victor. Her life free of Luther's dark influence.

Her life.

And she would protect it...protect that chance at happiness...at all costs.

Victor wrapped her in his arms and held her close.

Just where she wanted to be.

***

"Zoe..."

Her name was soft. Husky.

"Zoe, baby, I have a present for you."

Her eyes fluttered open. She found Victor sitting on the bed, holding a very large box in his hands. A familiar box.

"I just wanted to give you something," he whispered, "to make you happy."

She sat up in bed, holding the sheet close. She lifted the lid off the big, white box. Saw the feathers.

Her costume. He'd actually brought the costume? Her fingers slid over the feathers. "It's really nice," she told him, swallowing the lump in her throat. "But there's something else that makes me happy…"

"What?"

Her hand left the feathers and touched the rough stubble of his cheek. "You."

And she saw the love blazing in his eyes.

Victor leaned down and kissed her.

You.

###

A NOTE FROM THE AUTHOR

Thank you for reading MINE TO PROTECT. I hope that you enjoyed Victor's story.

If you'd like to stay updated on my releases and sales, please join my newsletter list www.cynthiaeden.com/newsletter/. You can also check out my Facebook page www.facebook.com/cynthiaedenfanpage. I love to post giveaways over at Facebook!

Again, thank you for taking the time to read MINE TO PROTECT.

Best,

Cynthia Eden
www.cynthiaeden.com

ABOUT THE AUTHOR

Award-winning author Cynthia Eden writes dark tales of paranormal romance and romantic suspense. She is a *New York Times, USA Today, Digital Book World,* and *IndieReader* best-seller. Cynthia is also a three-time finalist for the RITA® award. Since she began writing full-time in 2005, Cynthia has written over fifty novels and novellas.

Cynthia is a southern girl who loves horror movies, chocolate, and happy endings. More information about Cynthia and her books may be found at: http://www.cynthiaeden.com or on her Facebook page at: http://www.facebook.com/cynthiaedenfanpage. Cynthia is also on Twitter at http://www.twitter.com/cynthiaeden.

HER WORKS

List of Cynthia Eden's romantic suspense titles:

- WATCH ME (Dark Obsession, Book 1)
- WANT ME (Dark Obsession, Book 2)
- NEED ME (Dark Obsession, Book 3)
- BEWARE OF ME (Dark Obsession, Book 4)
- MINE TO TAKE (Mine, Book 1)
- MINE TO KEEP (Mine, Book 2)
- MINE TO HOLD (Mine, Book 3)
- MINE TO CRAVE (Mine, Book 4)
- MINE TO HAVE (Mine, Book 5)
- FIRST TASTE OF DARKNESS
- SINFUL SECRETS
- DIE FOR ME (For Me, Book 1)
- FEAR FOR ME (For Me, Book 2)
- SCREAM FOR ME (For Me, Book 3)
- DEADLY FEAR (Deadly, Book 1)
- DEADLY HEAT (Deadly, Book 2)
- DEADLY LIES (Deadly, Book 3)
- ALPHA ONE (Shadow Agents, Book 1)

- GUARDIAN RANGER (Shadow Agents, Book 2)
- SHARPSHOOTER (Shadow Agents, Book 3)
- GLITTER AND GUNFIRE (Shadow Agents, Book 4)
- UNDERCOVER CAPTOR (Shadow Agents, Book 5)
- THE GIRL NEXT DOOR (Shadow Agents, Book 6)
- EVIDENCE OF PASSION (Shadow Agents, Book 7)
- WAY OF THE SHADOWS (Shadow Agents, Book 8)

Paranormal romances by Cynthia Eden:
- BOUND BY BLOOD (Bound, Book 1)
- BOUND IN DARKNESS (Bound, Book 2)
- BOUND IN SIN (Bound, Book 3)
- BOUND BY THE NIGHT (Bound, Book 4)
- BOUND IN DEATH (Bound, Book 5)
- THE WOLF WITHIN (Purgatory, Book 1)
- MARKED BY THE VAMPIRE (Purgatory, Book 2)
- CHARMING THE BEAST (Purgatory, Book 3)

- DEAL WITH THE DEVIL (Purgatory, Book 4)

Other paranormal romances by Cynthia Eden:
- A VAMPIRE'S CHRISTMAS CAROL
- BLEED FOR ME
- BURN FOR ME (Phoenix Fire, Book 1)
- ONCE BITTEN, TWICE BURNED (Phoenix Fire, Book 2)
- PLAYING WITH FIRE (Phoenix Fire, Book 3)
- ANGEL OF DARKNESS (Fallen, Book 1)
- ANGEL BETRAYED (Fallen, Book 2)
- ANGEL IN CHAINS (Fallen, Book 3)
- AVENGING ANGEL (Fallen, Book 4)
- IMMORTAL DANGER
- NEVER CRY WOLF
- A BIT OF BITE (Free Read!!)
- ETERNAL HUNTER (Night Watch, Book 1)
- I'LL BE SLAYING YOU (Night Watch, Book 2)
- ETERNAL FLAME (Night Watch, Book 3)
- HOTTER AFTER MIDNIGHT (Midnight, Book 1)
- MIDNIGHT SINS (Midnight, Book 2)

- MIDNIGHT'S MASTER (Midnight, Book 3)
- WHEN HE WAS BAD (anthology)
- EVERLASTING BAD BOYS (anthology)
- BELONG TO THE NIGHT (anthology)

16653087R00177

Printed in Great Britain
by Amazon